Second Chances

The Road to Nineveh

Diane

Seek - Find - Embrace

Your Nineveh

SanDiego Elz

SanDiego Elizondo

Wasteland Press

www.wastelandpress.net
Shelbyville, KY USA

Second Chances:
The Road to Nineveh
by SanDiego Elizondo

First Printing – May 2012
ISBN: 978-1-60047-719-5

Printed in the U.S.A.

0   1   2   3   4   5   6   7

When Abraham was ninety,

the angels came to him.

They said,

"You're going to be a daddy."

And, Abraham believed.

Lord, let me be like Abraham,

and know your plan for me.

Let me be like Abraham,

And, Lord

I will believe.

ACKNOWLEDGMENTS

I must, first of all, acknowledge that this book would never have been written, but for the consistent words of the prophets spoken over me over for the past two years. Over and over again, strangers reached into the deepest recesses of my memory and reminded me of dreams long forgotten, creative dreams left in the dust of time while I was busy with the business of living.

Initially, I rejected each spoken word, but eventually came to realize that I was simply avoiding my personal Nineveh. If there are prophets in our time, and I am now convinced that there are, it is the duty of those of us over whom prophecies are spoken to analyze each spoken word and choose either to disregard the word or to embrace it.

Over time, I decided to accept the words spoken over me. That meant that I had to act on them. The pages that follow are the result of my decision to believe and act upon those words.

Accordingly, I must acknowledge and give thanks to all those people who have told me that I would write. I don't remember all their names, but I do remember three individuals who significantly impacted the creation of Second Chances: Carla Wood, Charlotte Stukenborg, and Mary Beth McElroy. Thank you each for helping me to find my Nineveh and to embrace it.

I must also thank my wife, Kay, for her constant support in the efforts associated with this project. Your encouragement and willingness to listen to this story on a daily basis as it was created one chapter at a time, sustained me throughout the creative process.

I would also like to thank Samuel Grammer for editing the manuscript that follows.

Finally, I must give thanks to God for giving me my story and the message associated with it.

CHAPTER 1

"Thank you, Lord, for the gift of flight and another day to fly."

As much as I enjoy flying with Joe, this little habit of thanking God every time I turn onto a runway and immediately upon landing gets annoying. It is not that I take Joe's prayers as any sort of comment on my abilities as a pilot. I don't. And, it's not because I'm an atheist who doesn't believe in God. I believe in God. I just want nothing to do with him.

As Joe is thanking God, I am easing the throttle to full and heading down the center line of runway One Seven Right in Abilene, Texas. At sixty-five miles per hour, I gently pull back on the yoke increasing the pressure I am already applying to the right rudder pedal. We break away from the runway. I apply a little forward pressure on the yoke, and stay low to the ground until my airspeed indicator says we are going eighty miles per hour. Then I relax the forward pressure on the yoke and increase the pressure on the right rudder pedal. With ten degrees of flaps deployed my plane climbs like a homesick angel. I barely turn the trim crank above my head, and we settle into an eighty mile per hour climb. We have been cleared to make an immediate left turn to the opposite direction.

I love taking off from Abilene. There is a great deal of activity in the early seconds of a flight here. We have to make a U-turn and climb quickly for the first two minutes of the flight. We will start our turn back to the north before we have even reached the middle of the runway and actually pass over the final approach area to a parallel runway, climbing as fast as my plane can to clear the airspace at Elmdale Airport, a mile east of the Abilene airport and then the windmill farm a little past there.

When we have cleared the windmills, I will lower the nose of the plane enough to keep from overheating the engine, and we will continue on up through the ground effect turbulence, which seems to surround Abilene year round, and on up to the smooth winter air which will take us home. The first two minutes of flight are bumpy and full of activity. I love it.

A 1964 Piper Cherokee 180 is a truck of an airplane. It weighs approximately 1200 pounds empty and can carry almost that much in passengers, gear and fuel. That is a great deal for a four place single engine airplane. In addition to having a high payload, the Cherokee 180 is considered tough, easy to fly and inexpensive to operate. These are the reasons I fly a Cherokee 180.

Before the day is over, I will gain more respect for the plane's toughness.

Over the past five years I have accumulated around fifty pounds of survival gear which permanently resides in the baggage compartment. I've never used any of the survival equipment before today.

My friend Joe and I are returning to Pogue Airport in Sand Springs, Oklahoma from Abilene, Texas where we have just dropped off my seven-year-old daughter to spend the week with her grandparents. She will spend four days with her mother's parents and then three with mine. Next Sunday my father will bring her to the Abilene Airport and we will fly back to Sand Springs. Rachel has been flying with me almost since the day she was born, and she loves flying. She loves flying almost as much as I do.

I am convinced that there are two kinds of people in the world. There are those who think of an airplane as a way to get from one place to another quickly, and there are those who are absolutely, totally and completely in love with the very notion of flight. Rachel, like her father, falls hopelessly into the latter category.

For me flight is a passion. I feel deep within me an incredible gratitude that in the entire history of the world, there has only been a little over a hundred years when men and women could actually fly like the birds, and that I am blessed enough to be living in that brief period of history. Rachel shares that passion. She will be a pilot. I'm sure of it.

Joe is a pilot too. He also has the passion. Most pilots do. I'm not sure how old Joe is. He won't say, but I estimate his age at eighty. Despite his age, Joe works as many as sixty hours per week, manufacturing specialty products for use in the oil industry. He is a tough old goat.

*   *   *   *

Joe and I met on six years ago on New Year's Day at a prayer breakfast for Alpha Aviation Mission Outreach, an organization which trains pilots and mechanics for the mission field. Six years ago I had considerably more use for God than I do today. Six years ago I was married to Rebecca, the love of my life. Six years ago Rebecca and I were deeply involved in our church, in our support of Alpha Aviation, and most of all in raising our beautiful baby girl, Rachel. Today, I am a thirty-year-old widower trying to raise my daughter by myself. Today I blame God for taking Rebecca away from Rachel and me. Today I don't have much use for God.

On that New Year's Day six years ago, though, things were different. Rebecca and I were giving serious thought to the notion of my leaving my employment and beginning study at Alpha Aviation.

I wanted to combine my passion for flying with my passion for serving God.

On that day, so long ago, Joe invited himself to fly with me and we have been flying together ever since. Over the past six years, we have flown to the world's largest fly-in in Oshkosh, Wisconsin three times, and we have made this journey to Abilene several times each year.

On the day we met, I was excusing myself from the prayer breakfast early, because I was going to fly over to a friend's hangar and ring in the New Year with a New Year's Day flight and some black-eyed peas. Joe said he'd like to come along. He did, and we've been flying together ever since. Although Joe owns his own plane, we always fly in mine. I suspect that Joe's medical certificate is not current, but I don't really know that.

Joe always helps pay for the gas. That makes him the best kind of flying partner. I also generally enjoy Joe's company. He is at an age where he says exactly what is on his mind without any thought to what others might think, and frankly that has made him fun as a friend. I remember that on that first flight, Joe criticized my airplane for being a tricycle gear airplane. He has a bias toward tail draggers. He criticized my landings as having obviously been made by someone who has never flown a tail dragger, an inexcusable shortcoming in Joe's opinion. Then, he proceeded to irritate everyone at the black-eyed pea luncheon. One pilot at the luncheon was giving rides in his home-built RANS Coyote. The plane was beautiful, but the pilot had built it with a tricycle landing gear instead of in the tail dragger configuration. Joe walked up to the fellow and pointing to the plane's front wheel said: "I see you decided to put a training wheel on your plane." We had a great time.

Rebecca and I laughed until we cried that night when I told her about my very first experiences with Joe. A month later I wanted to cry, but I couldn't. I was too full of anger to cry. This time Joe was there to console me on the sudden loss of my wife. Joe has been with me ever since.

* * * *

We left Pogue this morning, and expect to get home shortly before sundown. I don't like flying at night, and in winter it is very difficult to get from Pogue to Abilene and return home in the limited daylight hours of the season. So, we push the limits of daylight by starting the first leg of the day's flying shortly before sunrise. The trip is three hundred nautical miles in each direction as the crow flies (425 statute miles as the car drives). I average a ground speed of a little over 120 miles per hour and plan on three hours of flying in each direction. Actual time in the air is usually five-and-a-half hours, depending upon winds.

I am a stickler for what pilots call the sterile cockpit rule, restricting all conversation in the cockpit to the task at hand during critical phases of flight. Once we have reached our cruise altitude, and the plane is trimmed up, though, Joe and I drift into casual conversation. We have been chatting for a while. The subject has drifted to Joe's favorite topic: the Bible.

"Come on, Joe, seriously, you can't tell me that everything in the Bible is relevant and meaningful."

"Don't doubt me, Thomas." Joe is one of the few people who calls me Thomas. To everyone else I am Tom, but since the day I met him Joe has never called me anything but Thomas. Joe loves a good pun or hidden literary reference, and I usually pick up on them. This one flies right by me.

"Okay, then, Joe, tell me: What is the purpose of the story of Cain and Abel?"

"What do you mean?"

"Well, it seems to me that the story of Cain and Abel serves absolutely no purpose, other than to cause confusion about a great number of things such as who Cain was afraid of, who he married, where he went and so forth."

"In fairness, you're not really focusing on what's in the Bible are you?"

"What do you mean?"

"Your observation that the Bible account of Cain and Abel is a little vague on issues like where the people Cain was afraid of came from or whom he would marry is well taken, but I believe we should focus on the what the Bible tells us, not on what it leaves out."

"I don't follow."

"I'm just saying, you might do better to try to understand why we are told what we are told and why God does what he does, rather than spend time and energy trying to create and resolve different issues."

"I wonder, Joe, why does God do the things he does?"

If Joe catches my drift, he shows no clue.

I continue: "Even so, what's the point of the story? Cain killed Abel, right?"

"Right."

"Abel's blood called out to God, right?

"Yes."

"God confronted Cain, right?"

"That's right."

"Cain lied to God, God caught him in the lie, and God sent down a bolt of lightning and fried him on the spot, right?

This gets the desired chuckle from Joe. "No, God didn't fry Cain on the spot, but he did banish him."

"Okay, God banished Cain, but even in doing so he put a mark on Cain for his protection, didn't he?"

"For his protection?"

"Yes, God banished Cain, but Cain complained that he wouldn't be safe anywhere he went, because people would know what he had done, and they would kill him. So, the mark on Cain was meant to protect Cain."

"Yes, I guess that's right."

"So, tell me Joe, what did Abel get out of this deal?"

"We don't know what Abel got out of this deal."

"No, we don't, but we know what Cain got out of the deal. Cain killed his brother, and in doing so became the first murderer on the planet, and he got off Scott free. So, I rest my case, there is no point to the story of Cain and Abel."

"Keep thinking, it will come to you."

Now, Joe has turned the table on me. He's a smart guy. What is he seeing that I'm missing?

I return my attention to flying.

* * * *

We are crossing the Red River cruising at 9,500 feet above sea level. The air is clear, although by tomorrow we should have some "serious weather" as we like to say in Oklahoma. The winds are with us. We are making good time. We have been in the air about an hour-and-a-half and should be home in about the same amount of time from now.

There is no auto-pilot on my plane, and it takes constant attention to fly it. It is not difficult to fly, but I have to be constantly aware of my heading and altitude, making continual minute corrections to each. Right now the plane is trimmed up nicely. She is holding her altitude well, and I am doing little more than resting my left hand on the yoke to keep the wings perfectly level. Pilots refer to this as "flying with a heavy right wing." That's funny because Joe couldn't get to one hundred fifty pounds with his pockets full of rocks, and I outweigh him by a hundred pounds. If anything, we should have a heavy left wing.

The engine is turning 2500 revolutions per minute (RPM). That is full throttle, but at this altitude we are producing about seventy percent power, excellent for cross-country fuel efficiency. My fuel consumption can vary from seven to ten gallons per hour. I flight plan for ten gallons per hour, but know that I am flying much nearer seven right now. That knowledge puts a smile on my face.

I reach for the throttle to make a minor adjustment to the engine speed, and find it frozen in place. I can neither increase nor decrease my engine speed. The plane is running comfortably at full throttle, but the throttle cable should operate easily. I am concerned that it does not. I tell Joe.

This is a new one for both of us. The throttle is operated by a cable running from the instrument panel through the fire wall and to the carburetor. It is a simple mechanical device, and there is no reason it should not be working properly. Joe suggests that I check the friction lock. The friction lock is essentially a nut through which the throttle cable runs, and with which I can adjust the tension in the cable. I loosen the friction lock as far as I dare, but see no improvement in my situation.

Now I am thinking. What can be wrong? Did I miss something in my pre-flight inspection of the airplane? I have flown hundreds of hours in this plane. What is different about today?

Then, it comes to me. I did notice something wrong this morning before we left Pogue, and I chose to ignore it. Is that the problem?

* * * *

Before every flight in every plane, the pilot is responsible for conducting a pre-flight inspection of the plane. I did that. I started on the inside of the plane with an inspection of documentation and interior equipment. Then, I continued outside the airplane. I started on the left side of the plane, visually scanning the entire left side. I specifically looked in the fuel tank on the left wing and confirmed that it was full. I checked the Pitot tube and static port and made sure they were clear. I opened the cowling on the left side of the airplane and checked that side of the engine compartment. I found nothing unusual. I buttoned the cowling up. I checked the piano wire hinge on the left aileron to make sure it was in place and secure. I continued to the rear of the plane and checked the rudder and elevator.

I repeated the process on the right side of the plane, but before looking under the right side engine cowling, I got under the plane and drained a small amount of fuel from each of three fuel sumps into a clear plastic container. I checked the color, clarity and even the odor of the fuel. It was fine.

Finally, I proceeded to the right side engine cowling cover. I opened the cover, and laid the cowling door all the way open letting the right side cover lie back on the center section of itself. I checked the oil and found it to be one quart low. That's when I noticed that something was missing, something that as far as I know serves no purpose on the plane other than to give me a place to rest the oil dip stick when I add oil. There is supposed to be a prop stick on the inside of the cowling like that used on most foreign cars to hold the hood open. The prop stick is nothing more than a metal rod the diameter of a pencil and about eighteen inches long, which can swing down from the cowling cover to the frame of the plane to hold the cover open. The only time I've ever used mine is as resting place for the engine oil dip stick when I add oil. When doing so, I lay the dip stick parallel to and above the prop stick as it lies in its cradle. The prop stick keeps the dip stick from rolling off the cowling, while I'm busy using my hands to add oil to the engine.

The prop stick was missing this morning. It appeared to have come loose and fallen through the engine compartment to the ground. I added a quart of oil, replaced the dip stick, and began a search for the missing prop stick. I scanned the engine compartment with the help of a flashlight, and satisfied myself that the prop stick had fallen off during my last flight, or, more probably, landing, and had passed through the engine compartment to the ground. Since it serves no purpose in flight, I decided to deal with it later.

The plane is scheduled for its annual inspection tomorrow. I decided to deal with the missing prop stick then.

* * * *

Now, flying along at 9,500 feet, I wonder if the prop stick is actually somewhere in the engine compartment interfering with the free operation of my throttle cable. That must be it.

Based upon this hypothesis, I begin to consider my options.

We are within ten miles of an airport. We should land and address the problem, but we are one hundred miles from home. If we land, someone will have to come get us, and the plane will still be a hundred miles from its hangar. To top that off, a mechanic is scheduled to come to the hangar tomorrow to conduct the annual inspection of the plane. Why should I have to pay two mechanics to solve one problem?

The plane is flying fine. Whatever that prop stick is doing, it really isn't creating any danger, expect for the danger it will create when we try to land. If all the excitement, if there is going to be any, is going to occur at landing, I might as well be landing at my home airport.

This logic is called "got-to-get-home-itus," and it has killed many pilots. Nevertheless, I decide to go home.

Now, Joe and I talk about how we will land a plane with a throttle stuck full open. I decide to begin a long slow descent now by slightly lowering the nose of the plane. We can descend at a rate of about one hundred feet per minute and level off at about two thousand feet above sea level. We have plenty of time to lose our altitude, and a gradual descent will avoid the dangers associated with making a full throttle dive. I calculate that we will be at two thousand feet above sea level about twenty miles from Pogue. That is pattern altitude for our airport. We will maintain that altitude and fly a straight-in approach to runway Three Five. As soon as I have the runway made, I will lean the mixture to idle cut-off, killing the engine, slow the plane down by adjusting the nose attitude up, throw in some flaps, and make a dead stick landing. Now, I have a plan.

Joe and I agree that we have an interesting situation, but neither of us has any sense that we are in danger. We are correct that the situation is interesting. We are wrong about the danger.

As we fly on, gradually descending to our desired altitude, I begin to contemplate and rehearse the actual landing in my mind. It occurs to me that I may have an ace in the hole. The runway at Pogue is a mile long, and we shouldn't have any problem executing the landing, but if we do, I can restart the engine and go around by pushing the mixture to full rich.

* * * *

I recall that once when I was a student pilot on one of my first solo flights, I accidentally leaned the engine mixture to idle cut-off instead of pulling on the carburetor heat. I was in the landing pattern. The engine immediately shut down. Just as immediately I pushed the mixture back in, and the engine restarted. I never told anyone about that, but today it gives me some measure of confidence about our plan.

* * * *

Confident that I can execute the planned landing, I give some thought to increasing our odds of being found quickly if things don't go exactly as planned. Pogue is not a controlled airport. There is no control tower there, and we will be landing just before dark. We need to make sure that someone will be looking for us if things go badly. I tell Joe that I intend to contact Tulsa International when we are about twenty miles out, and tell them what is going on. When we are on the ground, we can let them know that we are safe.

We are getting closer to home by the minute, and although we are not afraid, it is starting to get a little tenser in the cockpit. Neither of us has ever contemplated, much less trained for a full throttle approach to a dead stick landing. Pilots train for engine out situations, not engine stuck "on" situations.

Sensing my growing anxiety, Joe reminds me: "Aviate, navigate, communicate." Less than a week ago we attended a pilot seminar put on by the FAA. The seminar was on emergency off-field landings. Joe is reminding me that many fatal flying accidents result from pilots losing their composure when things begin to go wrong. At the recent seminar we were taught to prioritize our actions in an emergency. The mantra was: Aviate, Navigate, Communicate. The first order of business is flying the airplane. Aviate. Pay attention to the basics of safe flight. Look outside. Watch your airspeed. Watch your attitude. We want to maintain a straight and level attitude as much as possible.

Next, we need to navigate. We must maintain situational awareness, and maintain our course.

Finally, we need to communicate.

We are still eighty miles from Pogue, but I dial in the approach frequency for Tulsa International on one of the radios. When I start hearing Tulsa's chatter clearly, I will begin the process of communication.

* * * *

Then, Joe yells: "Fire!"

CHAPTER 2

As the troubled Cherokee flies one-and-a-half miles above the quiet little college town of Shawnee, Oklahoma another drama is unfolding below. Turkeyneck Gibson and Squat Baker are about to graduate from their previous unimportant lives of petty crime into their new unimportant lives as dangerous criminals.

Turkeyneck and Squat have been friends of a sort for the past three years ever since each was responsible for sending the other to reform school.

They were each fifteen years old when they accomplished that interesting feat. They attended the same street school at that time, and although they really didn't know each other well, each knew he didn't like the other.

* * * *

On a Sunday night three years ago, Turkeyneck was engaged in his primary hobby, vandalism. Just for grins he had broken into a coin-operated laundry, and torn the place to pieces. He ripped the doors off every washing machine and dryer in the place and punched holes in every wall. Finished with his night's work and thoroughly satisfied with his accomplishments, he was about to leave the Laundromat and go home to get some well-deserved rest when a can of spray paint sitting on a shelf in a supply closet caught his attention.

He was able to see the can of spray paint because the door to the closet had been ripped off its hinges. An idea hit him, and he chuckled to himself. He took the can of spray paint, and painted a message on one of the inside walls of the business. The message read: "Squat Baker did this."

"Brilliant!" He thought to himself. Now he could go home and get some rest.

Turkeyneck was not as brilliant as he thought he was.

The following morning it took the police investigator for the Shawnee Police Department exactly one second to determine that Squat Baker had not committed the vandalism and about one second more to deduce that Squat Baker could probably tell him who had committed the crime.

The investigator, Janson Parker, took a tape measure from his car and measured the distance between the spray painted message and the floor. It was exactly six feet.

He finished his crime scene investigation, and drove directly to Squat Baker's home, a rundown frame house about a mile away. Squat lived there with his mother and six brothers and sisters. All the children were school-aged, and all should have been in school when the investigator arrived at their home. They were not. The entire family was home and apparently still in bed.

It was 9:30 in the morning when Mrs. Baker answered Janson Parker's knock on the door. She recognized him, and immediately launched into him with a barrage of verbal assaults. Parker asked to talk with Squat, and his mother started screaming.

"Why do you need to talk to him? He's a good boy. He's been home all night. He ain't done nothin'." At that very moment, Squat came walking into the room wearing a pair of gym shorts and a t-shirt, and rubbing the sleep from his eyes.

Squat was called Squat because of his short stature. In his bare feet he stood before Janson Parker clearly no taller than five feet two inches.

"Squat," began Parker "your mother says you've been home all night. Is that right?"

"Yeah, that's right. What's it to you?"

"You weren't at the City Laundromat?"

"Hell no!"

"I believe you, Squat, but I have a question for you. Can you think of anyone who might have trashed the place, and then written: "Squat Baker did this." on the wall? Someone really tall. Say somewhere around six-foot three?"

Squat though for just a second, and then answered: "Yeah, Turkeyneck. He hates me, and I hate him."

"Does Turkeyneck have a last name?"

"Gibson, I think. He goes to street school. He's a real jerk. It might have been him."

With that Parker excused himself. It took two phone calls to identify Turkeyneck as Richard Gibson. Fifteen minutes later Parker was talking with Gibson on the front steps of his aunt's home. He had recently moved to Shawnee to live with his aunt after he had been released from a reform school near Tulsa, Oklahoma.

Turkeyneck had been committed to the reform school when he was twelve years old for felony murder. Felony murder is a particular class of murder, which requires no intent to kill. If in the commission of a felony, a person causes the death of another, he can be charged with felony murder. For an adult, a conviction for felony murder can carry the death sentence. Because of his youth he was being treated with extreme leniency.

Parker immediately understood the nickname Turkeyneck. Richard was six feet three inches tall, just as Parker suspected he would be. He weighed around one hundred thirty pounds and had the longest neck and the biggest Adam's apple Parker had ever seen.

Gibson was transported to the police station, and advised of his rights. He was asked to explain the black paint on the fingers of his right hand. He couldn't. Then he was asked if he knew why Squat Baker would say it was probably he who had vandalized the City Laundromat.

Gibson was completely befuddled. How could the police already be talking to him? He decided that Baker had ratted him out, but he couldn't understand how Baker could possibly know it had been he who vandalized the Laundromat. This was beyond his comprehension, but he figured he knew a thing or two about Baker, and he was in a mood to punish Baker.

At the end of the day, Janson Parker had cleared the case of the vandalism of the City Laundromat as well as the burglary of a railroad car two hundred yards behind Baker's home.

Two weeks earlier, someone had broken into a box car on the Burlington Northern Santa Fe Railroad and stolen several cases of beer. Gibson had heard that Baker had been bragging about this theft, and he was eager to share this information with Parker.

It was not long until Turkeyneck Gibson and Squat Baker were both residing in a reform school near Tulsa, Oklahoma forming their now three-year-old friendship.

They never knew how Janson Parker had gotten on to them. They didn't know that Parker knew that when people write on a wall, they tend to write at their own eye level. Parker knew almost instantly upon seeing the writing on the wall of the Laundromat that five-foot, two inch Squat Baker had not done it.

He was looking for someone who was six-feet, three inches tall, and he was pretty sure Baker could tell him who he was looking for.

*   *   *   *

Today Turkeyneck and Squat have recently graduated from the juvenile justice system. They are contemplating their first major crime as adults. They are going to commit an armed robbery.

CHAPTER 3

Katie McElroy lives for her Sunday evening flights. Since the first week of December, Katie has only seen the sunshine on Saturdays and Sundays. During the week, she arrives at work at McCabe, Gibbs, Owens, Dexter and Jones an hour before sunrise and emerges at the end of the day a full hour after sunset.

She was not misled. She was warned that the life of a junior associate in any law factory was a hard life. She doesn't mind the hard work. She just misses daylight.

* * * *

Katie started taking flying lessons in her father's 1958 Super Cub when she was fourteen, had already accumulated two hundred hours before she soloed on her sixteenth birthday, and she flew another hundred hours before she took her private pilot check ride on her seventeenth birthday.

According to the law, a pilot can qualify for the private pilot check ride with as little as forty hours of flying.

Katie didn't take longer to get her license because of any lack of knowledge or skill. She took longer because the law also says a person cannot solo an airplane until his or her sixteenth birthday and cannot get a private license until his or her seventeenth birthday.

* * * *

Flying is her passion. It is also largely her secret. For reasons she never really understood, Katie didn't mention her flying in any interviews with McCabe, Gibbs, Owens, Dexter and Jones. The secret is not intentional, but the fact that her passion for flying has remained hidden from her colleagues at the firm somehow keeps it all the more special.

Katie has been in the Civil Air Patrol since she was a teen-ager, first as a cadet, and now as a member of an adult squadron. She holds the rank of Major, but since CAP is a volunteer organization there really isn't much pay differential between a Second Lieutenant and a Major.

There are thirty-three pilots in Katie's squadron. She is one of six who are qualified as Mission Pilots. The others are Mission Transport Pilots. Mission Transport Pilots can deliver airplanes, personnel and equipment where needed and can even fly communication flights, known as High Bird Flights, during exercises or actual missions; but only Mission Pilots fly the actual search and rescue missions for CAP.

* * * *

Today, Katie is flying a proficiency flight in a CAP aircraft in preparation for her annual CAP check ride. There are over a half million licensed pilots in the United States. Unlike the vast majority of those pilots who take one check ride in their lifetimes, CAP pilots take a check ride every twelve months. Consequently, there is only one flying organization in the world with a better safety record than CAP, and that is the United States Air Force.

Katie will fly almost two hours today at a cost of approximately sixty dollars per hour. That is cheap flying, but even at that rate Katie pays over six thousand dollars per year for the privilege of volunteering as a Mission Pilot for CAP.

There is a saying in CAP that a plane cannot take off until the paperwork associated with the flight weighs the same as the plane. Katie has just put the finishing touches on her pre-flight paperwork, has completed her pre-flight inspection of the Cessna 172 she will be flying, and is waiting for the final clearance from her flight release officer. She has dialed his cell phone number, and Lt. Decker answers on the first ring.

"Bill, this is Katie. The plane is ready to go."

Bill conducts a short safety interview with Katie, and concludes with a question. "Are you safe?"

"I'm safe."

I'M SAFE is an acronym used by pilots across the United States as a final check on their readiness to fly. "I" stands for illness, "M" for medications, "S" for stress, "A" for alcohol, "F" for fatigue and "E" for emotions. By responding "I'm safe," Katie has just acknowledged that she has conducted the self-evaluation reflected in the acronym and found herself fit to fly.

Bill responds: "You are released. CAVU."

CAVU is in the nature of a blessing, meaning I wish you clear air with visibility unlimited.

Katie enters her plane, and prepares to depart. Cleared to taxi, she proceeds to Runway One Eight Right, completes her run-ups and announces to the control tower that she is ready to depart. Cleared to depart, Katie enters and turns left onto the runway, pushes the throttle all the way in, and says a little prayer. "Thank you, Lord for the gift of flight and another day to fly."

CHAPTER 4

Marty Dixon is very busy today spending his anticipated inheritance. There is nothing on earth he enjoys as much as flying low and slow in his Piper Super Cub, and the lower and slower the better. The Super Cub is a powerful descendant of the Piper J-3 Cub. Most people probably think of the Piper J-3 Cub, a yellow high wing tail dragger airplane, when they think of a small private plane. For at least two generations of pilots that plane was their introduction to flight. Known as the safest plane in the world, because it could only barely kill you, the Piper Cub holds a special place in every pilot's heart, even if he or she has never flown one. The Super Cub has just as many admirers. Either will turn the head of every pilot at an airport when it arrives.

Marty's Super Cub is simply beautiful. It is white with a bold red stripe down the side of its fuselage, and it sports two giant balloon-like tundra tires. People who fly tail dragging airplanes refer to them as conventional gear planes, because the tail draggers came first. Pilots who don't fly them call them tail draggers, because when sitting on the ground the rear of the plane rests on a rear tire rather than in the tricycle configuration of more modern planes. They are more difficult to handle on the ground than modern tricycle gear planes, but they are simply breathtaking when they are sitting on the ground, looking for the entire world like they just want to jump up into the air.

Marty is thirty years old. His occupation is waiting. He is waiting for his inheritance, because as generous as his father is about Marty's flying, Marty will simply be able to fly more when his father is gone. With no specific ill will felt towards his father, Marty looks forward to the joyful day when he will realize control over what is coming to him; and he occupies himself with flying as much as he can afford to right now.

Everyone enjoys Marty's company. The hangar fliers at the airport love to hear him tell his stories. He is quite entertaining. He is also an excellent pilot with commercial and instrument ratings. His father paid for the ratings. His father pays for the flying. His father lives in hope that Marty will grow up, but in the meantime his father supports his son's habit. There are worse habits. Marty doesn't drink or use drugs. Those things would interfere with his flying. He is not a womanizer, although he certainly could be if he wanted to. He is presently between relationships. Women like

Marty, but they, like his father, tend to grow tired of his apparent refusal to grow up.

Today Marty is flying. He is flying low and slow, following the path of the Arkansas River as it meanders through northeast Oklahoma.

As he flies, Marty monitors two frequencies on his plane's radio. He is listening to Tulsa International Approach, and he is listening to Pogue Airport.

TULSA: "CAP Thirty-five you are cleared to turn on course for Pogue, advise when you have airport in sight"

RESPONSE: "CAP Thirty-five cleared to turn on course for Pogue, will advise when airport in sight."

Then, just a few minutes later he hears: "Tulsa, CAP Thirty-five, I have Pogue in sight, request VFR.

TULSA: "CAP Thirty-five, frequency change approved. Good day."

RESPONSE: "CAP Thirty-five, squawking VFR. Have a good day."

Marty thinks to himself: "a female CAP pilot, and she sounds young, and cute."

Marty is glad he is monitoring Pogue. He continues listening, and without giving his actions a great deal of thought changes direction, and begins to fly up the Arkansas River toward Pogue.

Katie has decided to begin her proficiency flight by doing some landings at Pogue. She enters the downwind leg of the landing pattern for Runway One Seven. The air is still, and she has her choice of landing to the north or to the south, but the convention in this part of the country is to choose the landing to the south when the winds are calm. She will fly a rectangular pattern entering her downwind leg from a forty-five degree angle at about midway down the length of the Runway.

She will fly parallel to the runway to the north until she is about a mile past the runway, then she will turn left and fly the base leg of her approach perpendicular to and approaching the extended line of the runway. Finally, she will turn left again on the final leg of her landing pattern.

Katie will have to demonstrate three different landings techniques on her check ride, and she decides to practice each right now.

Pogue is an uncontrolled airport. That means there is no control tower. Pilots landing at uncontrolled airports are responsible for their own safety.

A plane is not even required to have a radio to land at Pogue, but pilots who have radios use them. Pilots announce their intentions on a radio frequency assigned to the particular airport, and they listen for other pilots to do the same. They also keep an eye out for pilots who do not have radios.

Using the designated frequency for Pogue, Katie announces: "Pogue: CAP Thirty-five entering downwind for full stop landing Runway One Seven."

Katie has decided to begin with a short field landing. She will need to designate a point on the runway as her target, cross over the target, touch down within two hundred feed of that target, and come to a full stop as quickly as possible.

She chooses the one thousand foot marker on the runway as her target. The point one thousand feet from the threshold of the runway is indicated to by two broad white parallel lines painted on the runway.

This target represents the edge of the short field at which Katie is simulating a landing. When she is abeam the one thousand foot marker, she reduces power to 1,900 RPM and begins slowing the plane down by raising the nose of the plane slightly. She slows down to eighty miles per hour, and puts in ten degrees of flaps.

Flaps allow a plane to fly more slowly than it otherwise would be able to. As she turns onto her base leg, she slows down a little more, and puts in ten more degrees of flaps, announcing: "Pogue, CAP Thirty-five turning base for full stop landing Runway One Seven, Pogue."

Finally, Katie turns onto the final leg of her approach to landing putting in ten more degrees of flaps, and announcing: "Pogue, CAP Thirty-five turning final for full stop landing Runway One Seven, Pogue."

Katie is finished talking for the moment, but Marty is still listening.

"She does sound cute," he says to himself. Marty has been in position to observe Katie's progress through the landing pattern, and having heard her announce an intention to make a full stop landing, as opposed to a touch and go, he decides to land at Pogue himself.

Now Katie has to execute the landing. The plane is trimmed up, and she is flying at her desired air speed. From here forward she will make almost no adjustments to the plane's attitude until she begins her final landing flair. She will adjust her rate of decent by increasing or decreasing power to the engine.

If she has done everything right up to this point, those adjustments should be minimal. They are. Katie does little more than add a touch of power to get her almost exactly to her targeted landing spot. At the proper moment, Katie cuts power to the engine completely, pulls back gently on the yoke and lands within ten feet of her target. Immediately, she hits the electric flap switch taking out all flaps, and stands on the brakes.

"Not bad," she says to herself.

Katie doesn't actually come to a full stop. When she has satisfied herself that her landing has been successful, she releases pressure on the brakes and taxies to the first exit from the runway, announcing: "Pogue, CAP Thirty-five is clear of Runway One Seven, Pogue."

Just as she clears the runway, Marty announces: "Pogue, Piper 7777 is entering a left downwind for a full stop landing on Runway One Seven, Pogue."

Now, committed to making the landing, Marty is disappointed to hear Katie announce that she is taxiing back to Runway One Seven for departure.

Katie taxies back to Runway One Seven and holds short while Marty lands his Super Cub.

She waits, watches, and listens.

"Pogue, Piper 7777 is on final for a full stop landing, Runway One Seven, Pogue."

"He sounds cute," she thinks to herself.

Then she sees his plane and his landing. Both are beautiful.

Marty exits the runway and parks his plane. Katie enters the runway and takes off again.

* * * *

Like, Marty, Katie is monitoring two radio frequencies. On the first, she is talking and listening to Pogue. On the second one she is listening to the emergency transmission frequency. Although listening to the emergency frequency is not strictly required by regulation, most CAP pilots monitor the frequency when they are in the air.

Katie flies the landing pattern two more times, practicing first a soft field and then a normal landing. Each of these landings is a touch and go. Now she leaves the pattern for the west.

Katie flies to an isolated area where she will practice all the maneuvers she will be expected to demonstrate on her check ride.

Marty has now gone into the pilot center, commonly referred to as an FBO, at Pogue, and is in conversation with the attendant there. The attendant's name is Franklin. He is a retired local business man who works weekends at the airport. Marty and Franklin watch Katie's two touch and go landings, listening to her announcements over a speaker in the FBO. Marty comments that Katie sounds cute, and Franklin confirms that she is.

Franklin also mentions that Katie usually buys fuel at Pogue before returning to Tulsa International. Marty is in no hurry. He decides to hang around for a while.

About an hour later, Katie begins making her way back toward Pogue. She has one more procedure to practice, an emergency landing. Katie is flying at an altitude of 5,500 feet from the west to the east about four miles north of Pogue. She pulls the throttle back to idle. Then, she gently pulls back on the yoke until she is flying at seventy four miles per hour. She puts in trim to hold that airspeed, and announces on the radio that she is four miles north of Pogue on a long straight in approach for Runway One Seven, simulating an emergency landing. The airport is well within Katie's glide range. In fact, the difficult part of this landing will be to avoid going long on her approach.

Through the judicious use of flaps and shallow S turns, she brings the plane down toward the runway. Once again, she has chosen the one thousand foot marker as her target. When she is absolutely certain that she has the runway made, she puts in the final two notches of flaps and executes a perfect dead stick landing within five hundred feet of her target.

Katie exits the runway and taxies to the gas pumps. After topping off both wing tanks, Katie goes inside the FBO. There, she says hello to Franklin, and meets Marty for the first time.

CHAPTER 5

All pilots train for emergencies. Most pilots routinely practice making long gliding approaches toward off-field emergency landing spots. Pilots know, even before they pull out their checklists, the basic things to do if there is a fire in the engine compartment or cockpit, and what a pilot should do varies according to when the fire occurs.

A fire that starts while starting the engine is treated differently from one that starts while taxiing, and that is treated differently from one that starts in flight.

If an engine compartment fire occurs in flight, a pilot knows that he or she must first of all shut off fuel to the fire, second prevent the fire or smoke from spreading to the cabin and finally get the plane on the ground as quickly as possible.

* * * *

As quickly as the word fire comes from Joe's mouth, we are both working through our checklists. In fact, even as Joe yelled the word, fire, he was reaching for a printed check list in the map pocket next to his right leg. The check list, which covers all the routine and most not-so-routine matters we might expect to encounter, fills up both sides of a laminated eight-and-a-half by eleven-inch piece of paper.

Looking outside, I see that, in fact, we are streaming smoke from the engine compartment. I suspect that we have an oil fire, but we might have a gasoline fire. I reach for the mixture control just as Joe is reading from the checklist that I should kill the engine by pulling the mixture control to the idle cut-off position. I do so, and the engine stops.

By habit, I pull back on the yoke and trim the airplane for a glide at eighty miles per hour. I am aviating. I will revisit that air speed decision in a few seconds.

Joe walks me though the rest of the check list. I turn the fuel selector to the off position, turn off the cabin heat, and make sure all vents are closed.

As I look around at the ground for a suitable landing area, I simultaneously push the "nearest" button on my GPS. That button pulls up a list of several nearby airports. The nearest is twenty miles behind us. I don't plan on staying in the air long enough to go twenty miles, so I choose an open field about six miles in front of us. I point the field out to Joe. He agrees with my choice. I am navigating.

It is time to communicate. I dial in 121.5 on my radio, and make my announcement. 121.5 is the emergency broadcast frequency. I hope someone is listening.

"Mayday! Mayday! Mayday! Cherokee 7626 Whisky is twenty miles northeast of Shawnee with two souls on board. We have a fire in the engine compartment, and we are preparing to make an emergency off-field landing."

I am about to repeat my message when I get a faint, broken response. "Cherokee making Mayday call. Say location again, CAP Thirty-five." Joe and I recognize the CAP designation. Not only have we been heard, we have been heard by someone who can help us: the Civil Air Patrol. Hurray for the Civil Air Patrol!

I repeat my Mayday call. There is no further response.

Now I have got to get on the ground and get there in a hurry. Eighty miles per hour is my best rate of glide. That speed will keep me in the air longer than any airspeed I could have chosen, and it will get me to the ground safely unless the plane burns up on the way.

I am about eight thousand feet above the ground. At my current glide rate, it will take me more than sixteen minutes to get to the ground. That is too long. I can't simply dive for the ground though. The stress on the plane would be unbearable, and even if the plane survived the dive, it probably wouldn't survive the pull out. Neither would Joe or I.

I decide to pitch for an airspeed of ninety-five miles per hour, which will increase our descent rate some. Joe has been mostly quiet to this point, but he suggests that I use a slip to descend more quickly. I do so by inputting cross controls, right aileron and left rudder, and the plane settles into a ninety-five mile per hour controlled descent of one thousand feet per minute. We are in a slip moving toward our intended landing spot at an angle leading with the right wing of the plane.

I have cut my time in the sky down to less than eight more minutes. That is an eternity, but I take comfort in the knowledge that I will be able to recover quickly from this descent and land the airplane.

When I remove the slip, I will need to kick the nose of the airplane around to the right to prevent excessive loading on the landing gear. All pilots learn this maneuver before they are allowed to make their first solo flight.

There is still smoke streaming from the engine compartment, but at least I haven't seen any flames.

I have done all I can for the moment. I must now fly the plane to the designated landing spot.

Joe pulls his cell phone from his pocket. Then, he complains: "No reception." He lays the phone in his lap for the moment.

"Good idea, Joe. Keep trying. Also, why don't you pull up your map app and lock in our lat and long."

Joes tries again.

The field I have chosen appears to be a pasture. It looks to be about a half mile long and just about the same width. The pasture is surrounded by rough shrub-covered terrain. We should make it to the pasture with relative ease. In fact, I estimate that we will land about one third of the way down the length of the pasture, and have plenty of room to stop the airplane.

As we slip toward the ground, both Joe and I are searching for obstacles in the pasture. Neither of us sees anything, but we are still miles away.

*   *   *   *

Speed in an airplane does not feel like speed. It feels like a snail's pace. Even at altitude when I am cruising well in excess of a hundred miles per hour it seems to take forever to cover ground. That is an illusion caused by a pilot's extended field of vision over terrain. A pilot can see miles ahead of the plane. Consequently the airplane seems to creep across the landscape even though it is going more than a hundred miles per hour. Additionally, the land in most western states is carved out into one mile square fenced sections. It seems to take forever to fly from one section to another even though it is only a matter of seconds.

* * * *

While I am extremely concerned about the fire, I have absolutely no doubts about my ability to make a safe off-field landing in the pasture. I have never made an off-field emergency landing, but I have landed on many grass runways, and am confident in my abilities. Unless we burn to death on the way in, we will land safely. I can't think about death right now. I have an airplane to fly.

Time is creeping by ever so slowly. We need to get on the ground but we are still two miles from the pasture and more than two thousand feet above the ground. Joe says that his feet feel hot. That is a very bad sign. The plane appears to still be on fire, and we are a full two minutes from landing. Surprisingly, I am not in a panic. I fully realize that I may be at death's door, but I am not afraid. Perhaps the fear will come later, after we are safe. Joe begins to recite the 91st psalm. It is comforting. I ask Joe if he is afraid. He calmly answers, "No, this is not my time."

I think to myself that Joe has got to be eighty years old. Why isn't this his time, or for that matter mine? I decide to save that question for later.

Now, we are approaching the edge of the pasture. We are a little high and a little hot, that is we are going too fast. I straighten out our approach by leveling the wings and kicking the nose of the plane around to the right. At the same time, I grab the Johnson bar, which for all intents and purposes resembles a parking brake lever, and pull it all the way up putting in forty degrees of flaps. We drop in altitude, but we are going too fast. Now we are eating up ground in a hurry. Because I have trimmed the plane for a ninety-five mile per hour airspeed instead of the usual eighty miles per hour I am used to, we are going considerably faster than I would like to. A Cherokee is relatively easy to slow down, but we are floating, and it looks like will overshoot our runway.

Calmly, Joe says "Kill the flaps." As he is saying this he cracks his door open. That is the only door on the plane.

I push the button on the end of the Johnson bar, and lower the bar to the floor, removing all the flaps I had put in minutes ago. Instantly the plane settles down to the ground. We have landed. We have not crashed, not yet at least. We, however, are on a washboard ride, bouncing violently along the ground.

With the flaps out, I reach for my hand brake, and pull hard, pulling back hard on the yoke at the same time. The plane comes to a stop just inches from the tree line at the end of the pasture.

Joe is already getting out of the plane. I am simply amazed at his speed. He steps on the wing and then down onto the ground and disappears from my field of vision. I am right behind him.

As I am stepping off the right wing onto the grass, I am reaching to open the baggage compartment door, and realize that I have left the keys in the ignition of the airplane. I can't open the baggage compartment without a key. I turn back toward the front of the plane and see flames. I must have the key. In an instant I am back on the wing reaching into the plane grabbing the keys. My cell phone holster hooks on the top of the instrument panel and the holster and phone fall to the floor board landing next to Joe's cell phone. I do not notice.

In less than five seconds I am at the baggage compartment door turning the key, and lifting the door above my head. I lean into the baggage compartment letting the baggage door rest on my back, and I begin throwing gear out behind me. I hope Joe is collecting the gear. He is.

I feel the heat of the flames which are now growing. I have time to grab my twenty pound survival kit, our coats, a small tent, and two light weight sleeping bags. I see two aluminum chairs and grab them. That's all I can get.

Joe and I move away from the plane quickly. We move into the trees, but we can still feel the heat of the fire.

Still in the plane is our handheld radio, some tools and our GPS unit. I think to myself: "At least we have our cell phones." I reach for mine, and sigh knowing exactly where it is. I ask Joe if he has his cell phone. The look on his face answers my question.

We gather our belongings and move still further away from the fire. Joe smiles and says: "I feel like Jonah on the shores of Nineveh."

I respond: "Are you kidding me?"

Joe takes one of the aluminum chairs from me, opens it up and sits down. I do the same. We both laugh. We're camping.

We know we will be alright now. We survived the landing. People know where we are. We can't possibly be more than five miles from civilization. Help is on the way. There is not enough daylight left to risk hiking out. We'll pitch a tent; rest and either walk out or get rescued in the morning.

Now, I'm thinking about Rachel. I feel horrible for her. Then, I realize, she is at Rebecca's parents. Neither they nor she will know anything about this incident until it is all over. That thought gives me great comfort.

* * * *

We still have work to do, and not much daylight left. I start unpacking the tent, and ask Joe to start gathering firewood. The tent is a dome tent which goes up in seconds. I throw our gear into the tent and help Joe gather wood.

I was a boy scout, and am a good fire starter. I also have some cotton balls soaked in Vaseline in my survival kit along with some waterproof matches. The cotton balls are perfect for getting the fire going, and in a few minutes Joe and I are sitting in our lawn chairs, warming ourselves by the fire, enjoying a cool drink of water from two of the twenty-four aluminum water pouches in the survival kit.

We've looked at the energy bars in the kit, and decided we can wait until we are rescued in the morning to eat.

The plane has largely burned itself to the ground, and there is a large black cloud of smoke that can probably be seen for miles. Hopefully, the Civil Air Patrol plane is homing in on the smoke right now.

I give Joe a quizzical look, and ask: "Jonah? Really?"

Joe looks serious. "Yes. How do you suppose Jonah felt when he found himself spit up on the shores of Nineveh?"

"I don't know, Joe. I guess I've never given that a lot of thought. I've mostly wondered whether Jonah was eaten by a fish or whale, how he stayed alive in the belly of the animal, and things like that."

"Well, there you go again, Thomas, doubting everything and asking all the wrong questions."

CHAPTER 6

"CAP Thirty-five to Tulsa, I am on short final for runway One Eight Right. Tower, please be advised that I just received a Mayday call on 121.5 reporting a Cherokee on fire and making a forced landing northeast of Shawnee."

TULSA: "CAP Thirty-five, are you still receiving the emergency signal?"

RESPONSE: "Negative, Tulsa. I am too low to hear the Cherokee now."

TULSA: "CAP Thirty-five, would you like to go around, and see if you can hear any more?"

RESPONSE: "CAP Thirty-five, affirmative. I would like to go around the pattern again."

TULSA: "CAP Thirty-five, you are cleared for the option."

RESPONSE: "CAP Thirty-five, cleared for the option."

Katie receives the clearance to go around the pattern just seconds before she crosses the threshold of the runway. She proceeds with her landing until all three wheels are on the ground. Then she removes all flaps, pushes her throttle all the way to full and takes off again. As she clears one thousand feet above ground level, she hears the final words of Tom's second Mayday call: "... two souls on board, making an off-field landing twenty miles northeast of Sierra November Lima, Cherokee Seven Six Two Six Whisky."

As Katie proceeds through the landing pattern for the second time she continues to monitor 121.5, but she hears nothing more.

Katie lands her airplane and taxies to the FBO where the plane is kept. Bill Decker is there waiting for her. He is scheduled to take a flight in the plane immediately after Katie.

Katie parks the plane, and gets out of it. She hurriedly walks over to Decker, and tells him everything that has just happened.

"Bill, we need to fly out to Shawnee right now. Those people need us."

Bill reminds her: "Katie, you know we can't do that. We can't just run a Redcap mission without having been assigned to it."

Redcap is the term used by the Civil Air Patrol to differentiate between a training mission and an actual search and rescue mission. Katie has just returned from a self-funded proficiency flight. The Civil Air Patrol is the civilian auxiliary to the United States Air Force, and while its command structure intentionally mimics that of a military organization, it is in every respect a volunteer civilian organization. As in the military, however, everything must go through channels.

Even though Katie has heard the emergency broadcast, was in the air when she heard it, and is within a short flying distance from the suspected landing or crash site, she cannot just initiate a search and rescue mission under her own authority. Authority must flow down from the Air Force through the wing commander for the state and finally to the local units and individual people involved in the mission. Procedure must be followed.

Katie knows that Bill is right, but there isn't much daylight left, and the people in the Cherokee need help.

Bill suggests that they hurriedly run the information they have up the channels using their cell phones. While Katie is making calls, he is thinking. After a very few minutes, Katie comes back to Bill, and tells him that everyone who needs to be notified has been notified, and a Redcap mission will very likely be authorized by morning.

Bill tells Katie: "While you've been dealing with the bureaucracy, I've been working. I have just been cleared to practice conducting a route search for a plane that has gone missing between Shawnee and Tulsa. Incidentally, I've listed you as my Observer on this training mission. Do you want to go?"

"Absolutely! Let's go."

* * * *

A full crew on a CAP aircraft conducting a search and rescue mission would normally consist of a Mission Pilot who flies the plane, an Observer who sits in the right front seat of the aircraft and assists the pilot as necessary, and a Scanner who sits in the left rear seat, and acts as the recording secretary for the mission.

The Observer and Scanner also serve at the team's eyes. It is they who actually look out the windows, trying to find the missing plane. Observers and Scanners are not required to be pilots, but they often are. Both Bill and Katie have been qualified and certified to sit in any of the three positions during an actual search and rescue mission.

On this simulated search and rescue mission there will be only two team members. There simply isn't time to advertise for a third team member.

* * * *

"Katie, we'll have to file a flight plan. Can you handle that while we're rolling?"

Katie did not have to file a flight plan for the flight she just completed because she never got farther than fifty miles from her departure airport. The present flight, however, will exceed the fifty mile limit, and CAP regulations require the filing of a flight plan.

Katie handles the details of the flight plan using a different radio than Bill is using to communicate with Tulsa, and within twenty minutes of Katie's landing, she and Bill are back in the air flying toward Shawnee, Oklahoma.

Bill is in the left seat flying the plane. Katie is in the right, acting as Observer. Bill asks Katie to call the flight release officer on her cell phone, and see if she can get permission to land in Shawnee, just in case. She does so.

Because this flight has been created as a non-funded training mission, Bill and Katie will be responsible for the cost of fuel as well as an hourly charge for the use of the airplane. They will split those costs. It will cost Bill and Katie just under one hundred dollars each to practice looking for a missing aircraft.

As the plane leaves the traffic pattern for Tulsa International, Bill announces on the radio: "Tulsa, CAP Thirty-five is departing the pattern to the southwest towards Shawnee."

At this very moment, Marty is back in the air on his way to his home airport in Claremore, Oklahoma. Marty is monitoring the Tulsa frequency. He knows Bill and recognizes his voice.

"Bill, is that you?"

"Affirmative, Marty." Bill recognizes Marty's voice too.

"I met one of your pilots a little earlier. I think she's prettier than you."

"Well, Marty, Major McElroy is right here with me. Would you like to say, hello?"

There is no more interplane communication on the subject. This chit chat is not proper, but it is not totally uncommon either.

Bill smiles at Katie. Katie blushes, but only for a second.

Marty is a little embarrassed by the exchange that has just taken place, but then he thinks to himself that Katie *is* pretty, and that there's no harm in telling a pretty woman she's pretty. He doesn't dwell long on the subject, though. Marty is on a mission of his own. He has a lot of work to do tonight, if he is going to be ready for the excitement he hopes tomorrow is bringing.

Marty wants to get to his hangar in Claremore as quickly as possible. As the crow flies Pogue Airport is just eighteen miles from the Claremore airport, but Marty seldom takes the direct flight. To do so means flying directly over Tulsa airspace and talking with air traffic control in Tulsa. Marty really doesn't like to talk to ATC, and will sometimes fly twenty miles out his way to avoid having to do so. Today, though, he is on a mission. He wants to get home and do some work on his plane. Tulsa ATC will clear Marty straight through Tulsa and directly over the runways at Tulsa International, getting him home in a little more than ten minutes.

Bill and Katie's flight to Shawnee will take the better part of an hour. On the way, Bill and Katie discuss their plan. They are monitoring 121.5 on the radio, and will continue to do so. If the plane has crashed, the emergency location transmitter (ELT) will send out an alarm on this frequency. If the Cherokee pilot is trying to talk with them, he will also use this radio frequency.

The sun is getting near the ground in the west when Katie thinks she sees smoke off to the southeast. Bill agrees that it looks like smoke, and he is about to turn toward the smoke when both he and Katie hear the faint sound of an ELT transmission on their radio. Bill maintains his heading and the transmission seems to get stronger. Bill continues on his heading as the sun sets in the west. Neither he nor Katie can see any sign of the smoke or fire they saw earlier, but they can tell that the ELT signal is getting stronger. Bill maintains his course. Katie turns the volume on the radio down as low as she can and still be able to hear the ELT signal. If the signal goes away, that probably means they are flying away from it. If it gets louder, they are probably on the right track. After about five minutes Katie and Bill lose the signal. Bill turns the plane completely around and flies back toward Tulsa until the signal starts coming in again. Bill makes a steep 360 degree turn to the left. The plane's radio antenna is located underneath the plane. The plane's body serves to block the reception of the ELT signal when the belly of the plane is facing east. The ELT signal is not coming from the direction of the smoke. It appears to be coming from the west. Bill performs a steep 360 degree turn in the opposite direction, and gets the same indication. The plane must have gone down west of their present position.

Bill flies to the west. The signal gets stronger. Katie is checking a sectional map, and points to it.

"It looks like they tried to get back to Shawnee. The signal seems to be getting stronger the closer we get to the Shawnee airport."

Bill agrees with Katie's assessment and maintains his course. When they are over the airport, the signal is quite strong.

Both Bill and Katie know that many, if not most, airplane crashes happen at or near airports as pilots try to stretch their glide path to the Promised Land. They suspect that the Cherokee has gone down at or very near to the airport. Bill decides to land at the airport.

By the time they are on the ground it is full dark. They find the airport unattended. They do not have the authority to conduct any kind of search on the airport without permission. Nevertheless, Bill focuses his attention on the transceiver he is holding in his right hand. A transceiver is a handheld two-way radio many pilots carry as a backup to their plane radio. Bill knows a little trick used by CAP searchers across America. Not all pilots know what Bill is about to do, but Katie does.

"I see you've had some ground crew training," she says to Bill.

"Yes, I grew up in CAP," Bill answers.

Many people are surprised to learn that while adults fly the airplanes used in CAP search and rescue missions, most of the ground work is conducted by teenaged cadets. When cadets are very near to a signaling ELT transmitter, it becomes more difficult to locate the source of the signal with the equipment designed for the purpose of locating ELTs.

Bill is about to use a little trick of the trade he has known since he was a teenager in CAP. He removes the antenna from his transceiver and puts it in his pants pocket. He holds the transceiver close to his body. The transceiver is tuned to 121.5, and as with the radio in his plane, he has turned the volume down to the point that the ELT signal is barely audible. Bill turns around slowly in place listening to the signal of the ELT. The signal fades as Bill faces the runway and grows increasingly stronger as he turns toward a bank of airplane hangars.

Just then, a man in his early forties walks up to them, and asks if he can help them. He is a pilot who keeps his plane at the airport.

Bill introduces himself and explains that he and Katie are trying to locate the source of an ELT transmission.

The man gets a little red in the face and says: "Well I guess I landed a little harder than I thought I did."

Bill and Katie both sigh. They realize that they have chased the wrong signal. Most ELT searches lead to a plane that has just been parked in a hangar after having made a hard landing. The pilot confirms that he just put his plane in the hangar following a late evening flight. Bill and Katie walk to his hangar with him, the signal on the transceiver growing ever stronger with each step. At the hangar, they confirm the source of the signal: a Cessna 150 that has just experienced a little bit of a bounce in its landing. The pilot goes into his plane, and resets his ELT. The signal stops.

Bill reassures the pilot that all pilots bounce from time to time. Before leaving he asks if the pilot saw or heard anything unusual during his flight. He did not. Everyone shakes hands, and Bill and Katie return to their plane.

"What now," asks Katie?

"I guess we fly back to Tulsa listening to 121.5."

Bill asks Katie: "Were you in CAP as a kid?"

"Yes."

"I figured as much, when you commented on the little trick I used."

"Yes, I've used that little trick a few times myself."

"Ever use it on a real Redcap?"

"Yes, once," she answered. "I found what I was looking for too. I wish I hadn't."

"I'm sorry I asked," said Bill.

"Don't be. It's okay."

Bill and Katie don't talk much on the flight back to Tulsa. Katie is thinking back to when she was sixteen years old. She was on her very first, and only, real Redcap search and rescue mission.

* * * *

She and her squadron mates had trained for years for this opportunity, and now they were on a real mission. They might even save a life. A doctor had gone missing in his homebuilt aircraft. The airplane was a very light weight two seat plane that was actually ridden more than it was sat in. The doctor had inadvertently flown into clouds; or rather they had actually dropped down on him. At least that was the speculation. He had been missing for three days, and an ELT signal had been picked up by a CAP plane flying the doctor's intended route. The signal was not heard on two previous attempts, but now it was being heard and it appeared to be coming from an area of scrub oaks about a mile-and-a-half from the nearest road.

Katie and her team had hiked in and were near the suspected source of the signal. Katie was holding a transceiver, and she used the same little trick she had seen Bill use tonight. When she had turned about three fourths of a full circle, the signal became noticeably stronger, and her heart jumped. She almost ran to the top of a small crest, and then she stopped dead in her tracks. She simply wasn't prepared for what she saw. It took her a few minutes to even recognize what she was looking at. When she did recognize what she was looking at, she got sick.

The mission was characterized as a success, a "find" in CAP parlance. Katie's adult squadron members tried to help her understand that what she and her team had done had given the pilot's loved one's peace, but she really couldn't understand that.

*　*　*　*

"We've got to find these guys," she says to Bill.

"We will."

"Bill?"

"Yes, Katie?"

"Will you agree with me in prayer?"

"Yes."

Katie prays: "Dear Lord, somewhere out there are two people who, if they are still alive, are in a bad way. They need your divine protection. Please, Lord, we ask you to watch over them, comfort them and protect them. We ask for comfort for their loved ones and friends. Lord, those two people may be injured, and we pray for your divine healing of whatever injuries they may have suffered this evening. We do not know whether these people are ready to meet you, and if they are not, we ask that you reveal yourself to them.

For ourselves, dear Lord, we ask for wisdom, courage and strength to deal with the tasks before us; and not only for ourselves, Lord, but for every person who is about to be touched by the events of today. We come to you in agreement, Lord, knowing that you have promised that whenever we do so, our prayers will be answered. Thank you for all your promises. In Jesus name, we pray. Amen."

As they fly on toward Tulsa, Bill and Katie continue to monitor the emergency frequency on their radio. They hear nothing. There is nothing to hear, because Tom and Joe did not crash. They landed. They did not set off the ELT.

CHAPTER 7

Turkeyneck is driving, but Squat is in charge. He and Turkeyneck are sharing a joint intended to calm their nerves. He reviews the details with Turkeyneck. They will back the 1978 Monte Carlo up to the front door of the convenience store. The store has been carefully chosen because it is on the edge of town making for an easy getaway after the robbery. They will time their drive into the store parking lot for an exact moment when it becomes empty. They will get out of the car, leaving the engine running. As they walk toward the store each will pull on his ski mask. When they enter the store, Squat will do all the talking. He will walk up to the clerk, shove the gun in his face and demand all the money in the cash register. They will take the money, tell the clerk to lie down on the floor, and be out the door and on their way out of the parking lot in less than thirty seconds.

Squat estimates that they will get ten thousand dollars. He is a little vague on his calculations, but Turkeyneck thinks the amount sounds reasonable. The pair will be well on their way to Texas and ultimately on their way to Mexico before anyone even thinks that it might be they who have committed this perfect crime. Squat has convinced Turkeyneck that two men can live like kings for a very long time on ten thousand dollars in Mexico.

On their twenty-seventh pass in front of the convenience store, Turkeyneck and Squat finally find the parking lot empty. Turkeyneck pulls in and backs the car up to the front door. He immediately gets out of the car, and is pulling his ski mask on as he walks toward the front door. Squat is doing the same on the other side of the car. As the pair enters the store, Squat pulls a thirty-eight caliber Smith and Wesson revolver from his pocket bringing the gun up to eye level as he approaches the clerk.

The clerk is also the store owner. He has been robbed three times in the last six months. He is sick and tired of being robbed. For the past two and half hours he has been watching the same blue 1978 Monte Carlo driving back and forth in front of his store with the same two characters sitting in the front seat nervously checking out his parking lot. He has known for at least an hour what is coming, and he has known when it would come. It would come the first time his parking lot was empty.

Now the parking lot is empty, and the two characters in ski masks are entering right on cue.

Before the pair takes three full steps into the store, the clerk levels his own thirty eight caliber revolver at them and begins firing. He fires six shots in quick succession at Squat. Squat is the one with the gun. At the same time, Squat fires six shots at the clerk. The shooters are standing less than six feet from each other. Neither is counting his shots. Neither knows that his gun is empty. Squat stops shooting because he cannot raise his left arm, his shooting arm. The clerk stops shooting because he is lying on the floor in a pool of his own blood.

Turkeyneck looks first at Squat, then at the clerk, and finally back at Squat. Squat is still standing, but he is bleeding from his left arm. The robbers run for the door, and get in the still running Monte Carlo. Turkeyneck turns right onto McArthur Street as he leaves the store parking lot. As he is driving, he is examining his partner as well as he can. Squat has been shot in his left wrist, but he is also bleeding from high up on the back of his left shoulder. Turkeyneck figures correctly that Squat has only been shot once in the wrist and that the bullet has travelled up the inside of his arm and exited out the back of his shoulder.

Turkeyneck's ears are ringing from the sound of gunfire in the closed confines of a building. He yells loudly to Squat: "Looks like the bullet passed clean through you. Just a flesh wound. You'll be okay."

Squat does not respond. He is dead.

Things are not going well. The car passes through a long tunnel, and as it is exiting the tunnel, the engine sputters. Turkeyneck looks at his gas gauge for the first time today. He is on empty. He wonders if things could get any worse. Turkeyneck turns right into the first parking lot he comes to, and runs out of gas as he pulls into a parking space at the Gordon Cooper Technology Center. The place appears to be deserted. Turkeyneck gets out of the car, dragging the body of his partner across the front seat. He grabs the empty revolver, and puts it in the waist of his pants. Turkeyneck locks the car and walks away from it to the west. He scales a ten foot chain link fence and enters the Shawnee airport. The tunnel he passed through moments earlier passes directly under the runway at the airport.

There is not much daylight left, and Turkeyneck is hopeful that darkness will prevent the discovery of Squat's body.

Turkeyneck walks toward some airplane hangars to the south wondering if a car can run on airplane gas. When he gets to the hangars, he searches in vain for an unlocked door. Next he moves to what appears to be an office building just to the south of the hangars he has been trying to enter. He works his way around to the front door, and tries the door. It is unlocked. He enters as quietly as he can, and stands inside the door listening. He hears someone working in an office to his left, and quietly moves down the hall to some stairs on the right. Quietly, very quietly, he moves up the stairs. At the top of the stairs he finds a lounge. The walls are glass on three sides. He has a clear view of the entire runway side of the building. He also has a clear view into the office area below him. There appears to be one young man working. Turkeyneck watches and he listens.

After less than five minutes, he sees a small plane taxiing in from the runway. It taxies to some fuel pumps directly to the west of the building he is hiding in. The attendant downstairs walks out to the plane.

"Great," he thinks to himself. I'll wait until the plane has been filled up and force the pilot to fly me to Mexico. "We'll need full tanks to get to Mexico." Turkeyneck will make his move when the guy finishes filling up the plane. As the pilot is moving the gas hose from one wing to the other though there is movement on the tarmac. He gets down as low as he can and watches out the window. Two men walk up to the pumps from the south and enter into a conversation with the pilot and the man from downstairs. The man from downstairs returns to the building and proceeds to turn off lights and lock doors. He is leaving. The upstairs lights go out. He has turned them off from somewhere downstairs. He won't be coming up the stairs. The man leaves. Turkeyneck hears the front door lock from the outside.

The trio at the pumps talks for what seems to Turkeyneck like an eternity. Finally, the pilot gets back into his plane, and starts it up. He taxies toward a large open hangar about two hundred yards south of Turkeyneck's hiding place, and the two men from the car walk behind the plane. At the hangar all three men push the small plane backward into the hangar. Then, they stand there in front of the hangar talking some more. Turkeyneck waits.

Twenty minutes pass, and then the men all shake hands. Two men start walking back toward the parking lot on the east side of the building. Turkeyneck loses sight of them. The pilot goes into the hangar. The two visitors get back into their car and drive away. There is one more car in the parking lot. It must be the pilot's car. Turkeyneck decides he will make his move when the pilot gets to his car. He watches from his perch as the pilot closes up the airplane hangar and then starts walking toward the parking lot. Soon he will leave Turkeyneck's field of vision. As he is waiting, he hears the obvious sound of an airplane landing on the runway. The pilot stops dead in his tracks and looks toward the runway. Both Turkeyneck and the pilot are watching the plane.

The plane is a red, white and blue single engine plane, which to Turkeyneck seems to be very official looking. His heart goes up into his throat when he sees two people in green military flight suits get out of the plane. They are fiddling with some sort of radio. The pilot is walking toward them. Turkeyneck is nervous now. He wonders if the police are already looking for him.

After a few minutes all three people walk toward the pilot's hangar. They open it. The pilot goes in, and then comes out. Then the military looking people, a man and a woman, walk toward the official looking plane as the pilot walks toward his car.

Although he cannot see the pilot's car, Turkeyneck hears the engine when it starts, and hears the car drive off. The military looking people get in their plane and fly off.

Turkeyneck collapses into a recliner that faces directly onto the runway.

He will spend the night at the airport.

CHAPTER 8

Carla is not a worrier. She is starting to get a little concerned, though. It's now past six p.m., and she hasn't heard from Tom. The sun has set, and she knows that Tom does not like to fly at night. Tom has formed a habit over the years of sending Carla a coded text message every time he lands his plane when returning from Abilene: S&S&OTG. It means: safe and sound and on the ground. She checks her messages on the phone, just to be sure, and sees the message indicating that Tom had landed safely in Abilene this morning.

"Maybe, he's let the battery run down on his phone," she thinks. "Hopefully, I'll hear from him before I get to House Church.

Carla and Tom's dad attend a traditional church on Sunday mornings, but on Sunday evenings they meet with anywhere from twenty to forty other people in a private home for a service they call "House Church." Carla has been participating in house church since its inception five years ago. Tom's dad has been coming for about twelve months.

* * * *

Six years ago Carla attended a Bible study group which met weekly in a local Methodist church. Victoria Long led that group. The study group had been focusing on the book of Acts in the Bible. Victoria had come away with a sense that the modern church did not even closely resemble the Church in Acts. She became determined to attempt to replicate the Church in Acts. The result was House Church, which met every Sunday and Wednesday in Victoria's home.

* * * *

Carla drives on to House Church, and is disappointed that she does not hear from Tom before she gets there. She decides to leave her phone on, just in case he tries to get in touch with her. Once inside, Victoria and the others welcome Carla.

The time from six p.m. until seven p.m. at House Church is a time for an evening meal and fellowship. The setting is positively that of a home, rather than a church. People spread out between the kitchen, the living room and a more formal dining room, and eat and visit.

Shortly before seven o'clock, Carla's phone rings. It is not Tom's ring tone, but Carla decides to answer it anyway.

"Hello."

"May I speak with Thomas Delgado?"

"This is Mrs. Delgado, Thomas's mother, may I help you?"

The man on the phone identifies himself as a representative of the Federal Aviation Administration. It seems that Tom has failed to close his flight plan. It's probably an oversight on his part. Would Carla, please have Tom call Flight Service as soon as possible? The man leaves her a number.

Tom is in the habit of filing a flight plan when he flies to or from Abilene. He does not generally do so for shorter trips, opting instead for a less formal type of protection called flight following. With flight following, a pilot usually advises ATC when he has his destination airport in sight, and ATC simply releases him to unmonitored VFR flight.

A flight plan involves a slightly more complicated process. When flying with a flight plan, Tom calls Flight Service shortly before taking off and gives them the details of his anticipated flight. Those details include such things as the type, tail number and color of his plane; the number of people on board; the route to be flown; and the estimated time enroute. He also leaves two phone numbers with Flight Service: his cell number and Carla's.

Upon landing, Tom is supposed to call Flight Service and close his plan. If he does not do so within thirty minutes of his estimated arrival, the phone calls start. Flight Service is calling the secondary number Tom gave them. That means they were unable to contact him at the primary number.

Victoria can see concern on Carla's face.

She asks: "Is everything okay?"

"I'm not sure. Probably, but I'm not sure. That was the FAA. Tom has not closed out his flight plan. I really should have heard from him by now too."

With that, House Church kicks into immediate action. Victoria calls the group to gather around Carla. She briefly explains what she knows, and the group spontaneously begins to pray, lifting Carla and Tom up in their prayers. The prayers are all positive, thanking God in advance for his protection. The night's agenda is forgotten. Tonight will be a night of prayer.

The praying is not brief. Neither is it organized. Everyone is praying individually. Some pray out loud. Others pray silently. Still others pray in the Spirit. Some lay hands on Carla. Others lift hands toward Heaven.

Carla's phone rings again. It is still not Tom's ring. It is the man from Flight Service. He tells Carla, that he has just been notified that a Mayday call was received from Tom indicating that he was making a forced landing near Shawnee. He does not mention the fire. He may not know about it. Carla has flown with Tom enough to know that there are plenty of places to make a forced landing safely around Shawnee. She also knows that Tom only needs a space seven hundred feet long to put his plane down. She asks whether it was night time or daylight when the Mayday call was received. The caller checks his notes. Then, he checks his computer to confirm what he suspects to be the case. It appears that the call was received about forty minutes before sundown.

"Praise God," Carla exclaims.

A shudder of hope runs through the congregation.

Carla is on the phone for several minutes exchanging information with the caller. In addition to the information he gives her, he wants to know more about Tom and his passenger. Who is the passenger? What are the ages of both Tom and Joe? How many flying hours does Tom have? Is Joe a pilot? What pilot ratings does each of the men have? What is each man's health condition? What survival or communication equipment does Tom have on the plane? Finally, he asks about Carla. Does she need him to contact anyone for her? He does not need to do so.

Carla and the caller exchange various phone numbers, and each agrees to let the other one know if he or she learns anything. The call ends, and Carla reports to her congregation.

Again, the group breaks into prayer. Again, the prayers are all positive prayers of thanksgiving. Again, the praying goes on for a long time.

CHAPTER 9

Marty lands at Claremore Airport and taxies to a bank of hangars located on the east side of the runway. Each hangar is fifty feet by fifty feet square. They are uniform in design, but each is owned by an individual. The land is leased from the Airport Authority on long term leases. Marty's hangar is on the front row of four rows of hangars. The hangar looks out directly onto the runway.

As Marty nears his hangar, he pushes a button on what appears to be a garage door opener Velcroed to the instrument panel, and the overhead door to the hangar opens. Marty taxies directly into the hangar and exits the plane. At the rear of the hangar is an efficiency apartment. Marty goes into the apartment, fixes a sandwich, and sits down to watch the evening news on television. Most of the hangars have just such an apartment in them. No one actually lives in any of the apartments, but a pilot arriving late or planning on leaving early may spend the night in his apartment.

Marty is going to be working on his plane tonight, getting ready for tomorrow. He wants to catch the evening weather report to make sure everything is still a go.

* * * *

Meanwhile, Joe and I are sitting by the fire discussing the day's events. We've had quite an adventure. I realize now that the prop stick I was so concerned about could not have caused the fire in the engine compartment. The frozen throttle was a symptom of a more serious problem. It was the never the real problem. I made a horrible mistake in not landing at Shawnee, and now I am sitting in a field looking at the burned out hull of my airplane, waiting to be rescued. I could have killed myself and my friend. I'm not very happy with myself right now.

Despite the events of the day, though, Joe and I are actually feeling pretty good right now. We realize that while we did some things very wrong, we did others very right.

"Kill the flaps?" I ask Joe. "Where did you learn that one?"

"You liked that one did you?"

"Yes, I did. I wouldn't have thought of it."

Joe explains: "You know I've got that place up on the grass strip in Cookson. Well, that's a pretty short runway, and it's set up where you try to land uphill to the north and take off downhill to the south.

Really, you always land and take-off that way unless the winds are just really strong. Well anyway, pretty often you will find yourself landing with a bit of a tail wind, which causes you to land long and even run long on your roll out. It's pretty important to get down quickly. I've learned from experience that when you're just inches from the ground, you can take out whatever flaps you have in. That, of course, reduces your lift, and the plane just settles down, like yours did today."

"Thanks for the tip, Joe. I'll keep it in mind just in case I ever have to land a burning airplane in a hurry again."

"By the way," I continue "You were pretty cool up there today. What did you mean when you said it wasn't your time?"

"Just that. I know I have some unfinished business God has in store for me. I'm ready when he's ready for me, but I know there's still something I've got to do. How about you, Thomas, are you ready?"

This is a sore subject for me. I blame God for taking Rebecca away from me. I was saved in a Baptist church many years ago, but I turned my back on God when Rebecca died. I'm not much inclined to give him much thought these days.

I tell Joe: "Joe I know that I've been saved, but I don't really think God has much to do with what goes on here on earth while we are living."

"Thomas, I'm glad that you are right with God, but if you don't mind me telling you so, I think you're cheating yourself out of a lot of the blessings that are available to you right now in this lifetime."

I am about to respond, when we both hear something and look up. We hear the unmistakable sound of a small airplane approaching from the north. We can tell from the sound that the plane is a single engine plane. Joe spots it first. It is about a mile northeast of us, and it is very low. It could be the Civil Air Patrol plane I talked with earlier. It's not quite dark yet. Surely the pilot sees the smoke rising from my still smoldering airplane. It must be the CAP plane. She appears to be flying directly toward us. We are waving wildly. The plane does a three hundred and sixty degree turn to the left, then to the right. They must see us!

Then, to our dismay, the plane makes a right turn and flies off to the west. Did they see us? If so, why did they leave? Shouldn't they be directing someone on the ground in to get us?

We find our way back to our lawn chairs and sit down. I remind myself that I just need to chill. We can walk out of here in the morning. It's not like we're in some remote wilderness. At first light, we'll just walk out of this place.

Joe says he thinks he's hungry after all. We each eat about a third of a twenty-four hundred calorie energy bar. It's not good, but it's not awful either.

I know that we are about to get back to where we left off in our conversation, and I am feeling a little awkward about it. I've got a pretty good idea where Joe is heading and I'm not interested in it. I walked to the front of a Baptist church twenty plus years ago and got baptized. I'm saved, and that's that. Joe is about to go where others have tried to go with me, telling me that there is much more to being a Christian than just accepting Jesus as your savior. I know his philosophy. God wants to be an intimate part of your life in everything you do. Jesus didn't just die for you sins. He died for your healing and your prosperity. Okay, that's fine for Joe, and Mom, and whoever, but I know better.

I know that bad things happen to good people and good things happen to bad people every day. So, I don't want to knock what Joe and the others believe, if it helps them get through the day. I just don't want it pushed off on me. Fortunately, there is a diversion moving in our direction, and I will be spared the rest of the conversation.

Sometime after sunset, another low-flying airplane approaches from the same direction the first plane took as it was leaving. This time we can't see the plane, but we can see its wing clearance lights. It is obviously low, and just as obviously flying slowly. We don't get excited this time though. We know the plane can't see us, but the plane is low enough to divert us away from our conversation.

It's early, but we're both tired. We've had a hard day. We decide to turn in. The ground is hard, but at least we have actual sleeping bags to sleep in. I look through the emergency kit, and find a couple of interesting items. I find aluminum blankets designed to help preserve body heat. They are essentially aluminum foil sheets. We each take one. I also find my wind-up radio. We take turns cranking the radio up for about five minutes, and then turn it on. We tune in a nearby radio station, just in time to get a weather report. The report calls for snow, and lots of it. The announcer is talking about feet of snow, not just inches. That's crazy. It doesn't snow like that in Oklahoma.

Joe and I agree that the weather men in Oklahoma make a living out of exaggerating snow possibilities. There is no such thing as feet of snow in Oklahoma. To be safe though, we decide on some precautions. First, we will bring as much firewood as we can into the tent with us for the night. That will keep it dry. Second, we will take turns getting up through the night to check on the tent. We don't want it to be collapsed by snow accumulations.

Joe has an alarm on his wrist watch. He sets it to go off every hour, and we turn in. Until midnight every alarm is a false alarm, except that the wind is now clearly coming in quite strongly from the north. At one o'clock, though, Joe wakes me, and says we are getting real snow. Fortunately, we've each had couple of hours of sleep by this time, because we are now in for a long night.

Neither of us has ever seen snow come down like it is right now. It is coming down heavy, and the wind is blowing it like crazy. We work through the night, shaking it off the tent. It is also drifting against the north side of the tent. We can't keep up with the snow. We take turns standing outside the north side of the tent, trying to shovel the growing snow drift away from the tent. If the drift collapses the tent, we will likely freeze under the snow.

I am amazed by Joe's strength and stamina. He matches me step for step in our battle against the snow. I'm not sure when, but at some point we realize that our shoveling efforts have paid off. While we have not been able to stop the snow drift, we have changed its shape and height. We have actually created a drift on the north side of the tent that rises higher than the top of our tent, and although it butts right up to our tent, it is not putting pressure on the tent. We realize that this drift will now actually protect us. We go back into the tent. I light an eight hour candle from the emergency kit, hoping it will help warm the tent. It does.

Joe and I are spent. We each drag an aluminum blanket into our sleeping bags, wrap up and go to sleep. When morning comes, we arise to an entirely different landscape. It is still snowing and the snow is at least eighteen inches deep in every direction. We can't really estimate the depth of the drifts, but they are frightening. We're not going anywhere right away. No one will be coming our way either. The clouds are just too low for anyone to fly VFR. There will not be any search and rescue missions until the skies clear. At least, I think to myself, we have plenty of food and water.

Joe and I clear the snow immediately in front of our tent which is facing the south. We bring out some wood and start a small fire. The fire is small and does not last a very long time, but it encourages us greatly.

Joe is singing to himself: "When Noah had drifted on the sea many days. He searched for land in various ways."

"Joe," I ask "are you okay?"

"Yes, I was just thinking about how great and merciful our God is. He's given us an ark in which to ride out this storm and plenty of provisions too."

I really agree with Joe, to a point, but I can't resist taking the bait.

"Well, you know Joe, not everyone would agree with your assessment that God was very merciful, when it comes to that whole ark business."

We go into the tent as we continue our conversation. I want to go after Joe on the whole issue of whether there really was an ark, but for the moment I decide to give him that one, and focus on the people who didn't get on the ark.

"You see, Joe, there might have been a few people and animals who survived that flood, but there were plenty more who didn't. God doesn't seem very merciful to me. He seems pretty mean, don't you think?"

CHAPTER 10

There is going to be a search and rescue mission tomorrow, and Katie is determined to be on the airplane, preferably sitting up front in the left seat, but she will accept any slot. She has some phone calls to make. First on the list is her squadron commander, Lt. Mark Jacobs. She calls him on her cell.

"Hi, Mark. This is Katie."

"Hello, Katie. That was good work you did today. That's why we monitor 121.5."

"Thank you, Mark. Do you know if there has been approval for a Redcap tomorrow?"

"It looks, likely. Have you checked your e-mail? I sent out a request for squadron members to confirm their availability about an hour ago."

"Oh, no! I was flying with Bill Decker. I'm just checking phone messages and e-mails right now. Have you filled all the slots?"

"The scanner position is still available. Do you want it?"

"Yes, I'll take it. Please don't give it to anyone else."

"Don't worry, Katie. The position is yours. I hope to have permission for you all to take off around sunrise. Will you be available that early?"

"I will, even if I have to spend the night at the airport."

"Okay, then, stand by, and keep your cell phone close by."

"Thanks Mark. I will. Good night."

"Good night, Katie."

Scanner isn't what Katie wants, but at least she'll be participating. There is a problem, though. Tomorrow is Monday, a work day. The partners in the firm don't even know Katie is in the Civil Air Patrol. Will she be able to get the day off?

Katie rehearses her lines in her head, and then she dials Marvin Owens, home number. Owens is her supervising senior partner at the firm. Owens answers the phone himself.

"Hello, Mr. Owens, this is Katherine."

"Yes, Katherine. How are you?"

"I'm fine, thank you, and yourself?"

"I'm doing well, Katherine. What can I do for you?"

Katie, ("Katherine" at the firm), spends the next several minutes explaining a great deal to Mr. Owens. It is as if she is confessing to a secret life. Owens listens carefully, and even seems genuinely interested when she tells him about the Mayday call and the rest of the events of the day.

"My, you've had quite an exciting day haven't you?"

"Yes Sir."

"And now, you want to take off tomorrow to go for an airplane ride, is that about it? You know Katherine, we pay you a lot of money, and we expect a lot for what we pay. It's not that I'm unsympathetic. It's more that I think that this *is* the sort of thing that is better left to the professionals."

"With all due respect, Mr. Owens, the Civil Air Patrol is the professionals in this situation. This is what we train for. I have been training for this opportunity since long before I ever even thought of becoming a lawyer."

"Katherine, I'm sorry, but you are needed at the firm. I am just going to have to deny your request. I'll see you bright and early in the morning at the office. Good night."

"Good night, Sir."

Katie is fuming. She doesn't know when she's ever been so angry. This just isn't right. She's angry, because she knows that this all about billable hours to the firm. She is expected to bill two thousand hours a year for the firm. The firm charges its clients one hundred fifty dollars per hour for the work Katie performs. She is paid a little under one hundred thousand dollars a year, while she earns the firm three hundred thousand dollars. Can't they give up one day of billing?

She knows she should call Mark Jacobs immediately and cancel her notice of availability, but she doesn't call him. She is going to call in sick tomorrow. Even junior associates are entitled to a sick day. She knows her decision might cost her her job. She knows she is making a poor decision.

Right now, Katie has some preparations to make. She has already decided that she will spend the night on one of the couches upstairs in the FBO. She's going to need some toiletries. There is a discount store a couple of miles from the airport. She heads that way.

An hour later, Katie is settling into her abode for the night. Before turning in she checks the computer in the pilot's lounge. It seems that there is a massive snow storm headed her way. It is coming a day earlier than previously expected, and is bringing more snow than people have ever seen in this part of the country. This is not good.

Just as Katie is about to turn in for the night, Bill Decker comes up the stairs. Katie is surprised to see him. He is not surprised. He saw her car in the parking lot.

"I see great minds think alike, Katie."

"I guess so," she responds. "Why are you here?'

"Same as you, I suppose. I'm expecting the roads to be closed tomorrow. If they are, I'll be here and ready to go. What's your story, Katie?"

"I'm already booked as the Scanner for tomorrow's anticipated mission, but I didn't know you were on the mission."

Bill says: "I'm not scheduled for the mission, but I suspect there may a vacancy if the weather lives up to expectations."

"You certainly are an optimist, aren't you?"

"I guess so."

"Well, you can take the other couch. I have dibs on this one. And, you better not snore."

"Sounds good to me. Good night."

"Good night."

Bill and Katie wake in the morning to more snow than either of them has ever seen.

Katie says: "I don't think we're in Kansas anymore, Toto."

Bill chuckles.

Right now, Katie is feeling sick to her stomach. She realizes how terrible the decision she made last night was. They don't mess around at the firm. She was wrong in thinking she might lose her job. There is no might to it. She will lose her job. What was she thinking?

Maybe it's not too late. Maybe she can still get to work. Sure she'll be late, but that's to be expected with this weather. "Please Lord, she prays. Get me out of this mess."

Out of habit, Katie is checking her e-mails as she is contemplating a way out of the grave she has dug for herself.

There is a firm-wide e-mail from the senior partner in the firm. She opens it and reads: "Due to unprecedented snow fall in the area, and the closure of virtually all roads and government offices in the eastern part of the state, the offices of the firm will be closed Monday and Tuesday. All attorneys and staff should expect to return to work on Wednesday, and be prepared to work Saturday and Sunday to make up for the lost time. Please acknowledge receipt of this e-mail."

Immediately, Katie types: "message received" and presses "send."

CHAPTER 11

Joe and are I waiting to be rescued. Our situation has changed drastically. We expected to get up this morning with either of two acceptable options before us. We could either walk out or be rescued. Both alternatives vanished in the night.

The option of walking out is simply too dangerous now. We don't know which direction to walk in. We don't know the terrain. The snow is too deep. It is too cold. It could start snowing again.

We are not comfortable, but we are secure. We have shelter and ways to keep out of the weather and stay dry. We will have to stay put for the time being.

The option of being rescued is also not very likely for the moment. The ceiling is just too low. The clouds are going to have to be at least fifteen hundred feet above the ground before any rescue plane can come looking for us. Right now the clouds appear to be hovering at about three hundred feet.

We are discussing our priorities. Joe thinks we should use the daylight hours to gather more firewood. I agree, but I also think we should be taking some actions to increase our chances of being found. What actions I just don't know right now. We have to think. While we are thinking, we will gather wood.

We are camped on the edge of a thicket of small trees. Yesterday we gathered dead wood from the ground, but all the dead wood is now covered by snow. We decide to try breaking small branches off the trees. It is a tough go, but we spend about an hour breaking off branches and dragging them back to the tent. We are working at a steady rate, but we are trying to not get overheated or even to break a sweat. After an hour we retreat to the tent to rest and have lunch. Lunch is the same as dinner last night: one third of an energy bar each.

After lunch we start back after fire wood, but decide to work in twenty minute shifts with twenty minute rest periods between them. This goes on for about two hours, and we are satisfied that we have enough wood for the day.

During all this labor, we made no attempt to restart our fire, which we really can't even locate now. The next order of business is to clear a pad for our fire. We have no tools. We have to shovel snow with our bare hands, and the going is very slow. We have to rest frequently, and go into the tent to warm ourselves.

After much effort, we clear a small pad directly in front of our tent. The pad is about a foot wide as it leaves the tent and expands out to a little over three feet wide at its largest point. We gather some of the dry wood from inside the tent and start a small fire. We have taken as much of the newly gathered wood into the tent as we can. We sit inside the tent, and tend the fire by throwing pieces of the recently gathered wet wood onto the fire. We have to keep the fire small for fear of burning down our tent. Still, it produces some welcome warmth.

There is nothing comfortable about our situation, but we believe we will survive another night out.

As we sit and talk. We talk about how to become more visible. Joe thinks we should carve SOS in the snow. I agree that it is a good way to be found, but argue that we just don't have the tools we need. We would freeze our hands off before we could make letters large enough to be seen from the air.

We don't come up with an idea.

The waiting is hard. The ground is hard. We are quite uncomfortable. But, we know that all we can do right now is wait. So, we wait.

We wait throughout the daylight hours, only getting out to answer nature's call. I note to myself that my next survival kit will have toilet paper in it.

CHAPTER 12

There are no windows in the apartment in Marty's hangar. He won't know until he opens up his hangar whether he'll be having his anticipated adventure today. Still, he demonstrates a fair amount of patience as he showers, shaves, dresses, and eats some cold cereal for breakfast. Only after he is ready to meet the day, with a fresh cup of coffee in hand, does Marty venture out into the hangar. He could open the personnel door on the southwest corner of the hangar and peek outside, but he opts for a more dramatic approach. Marty walks from his apartment in the rear of the hangar to the fifty foot overhead door facing the runway. He pushes a button and the door slowly lifts straight up about six inches. Then it attempts to swing out and up, but it can't. From inside the hangar, Marty can see that the door is being blocked by snow. He quickly hits the "down" button, and goes to the personnel door. The personnel door opens to the inside, and it is good thing, because when Marty opens the door he is faced with a four foot snow drift against the opening for the personnel door.

There is snow and plenty of it. Marty works his way through the snow to the front of the hangar, just a few feet away, finds a three foot snow drift blocking the overhead door. He has his work cut out for him.

Marty smiles a big smile, walks back around to the personnel door and looks back inside the hangar at his beautiful Super Cub, which is sitting on snow skis.

Last night Marty took the balloon like tundra tires off his plane and replaced them with snow skis in anticipation of snow. His work was not in vain.

Now, Marty looks back outside and up. He realizes just how low the ceiling is. It is too low to even allow him to practice flying in the landing pattern. Oh well, it won't stay low forever. Right now he needs to dig out of his hangar.

Marty has a snow shovel handy and he begins to clear a path from the personnel door to the front of the hangar. He doesn't have to clear the whole apron in front of the hangar, but he must move enough snow for the door to open. That takes almost an hour. Then, he starts to work on a makeshift ramp from the edge of the snow he has cleared toward the west. The ramp is just wide enough to accommodate both skis on the main gears of his plane, and the slope is gentle enough to allow the plane to drive over it without excessive propeller speed.

As Marty shovels the snow, he carefully studies its consistency and depth. It is deeper and softer than he expected. Both characteristics will complicate his plans. Hard packed snow would be easier for his purposes, but he can make do. Soft deep snow will present the possibility of sinking and getting stuck. Once he is outside and moving he will need to keep moving.

The sky has still not cleared, but that is okay. Marty actually has plenty he can do without ever leaving the ground. He mentally plans his next moves. Marty decides that it will be too difficult to pull the plane out of the hangar, so he decides to drive it out. He pulls the plane to the very edge of his snow ramp and then a little farther until the skis are both on the ramp.

Now, Marty walks all through his hangar making sure there is absolutely nothing that can be blown around by the prop wash when he starts the plane's engine. Anything that weighs less than twenty pounds gets carried into the apartment.

Marty climbs into the cockpit of his Super Cub, and does something he has never done before. He starts the engine inside the hangar. As soon as the engine starts, he gives it enough power to start up the ramp. It takes more power than he anticipated. Using short burst of power, Marty negotiates the ramp and immediately starts a wide turn to the left. He is blowing snow like a snow blower, and knows that he cannot stop. There is no one else moving on at the airport, and there won't be. Marty has the whole place to himself. Still, he is monitoring the airport frequency. He knows there will be no efforts to clear the runway today. There is just too much snow. He travels south the entire length of the runaway which is just over a mile and makes a wide turn to the right onto the actual runway. He listens to the radio and watches for traffic even though he knows there will be none. He even announces his position as he enters the runway and taxies the entire length of the runway from south to north. At the north end of the runway, Marty makes a wide left turn which brings him all the way back to the runway facing south. He runs the length of the runway again, this time to the south, always announcing his actions and always listening just in case. Marty repeats this process at least six times in each direction being careful to make new ruts with his skis with each pass. Marty is preparing the runway for when the sky clears and he is able to fly. He is packing the snow on the runway.

When he is satisfied that the runway is sufficiently packed, he taxies back toward his hangar stopping at the edge of his makeshift ramp. Marty gets out of his plane, and manually pulls the plane down the ramp and into the hangar. The hangar is large enough that Marty can spin the plane around and he does so. He closes the hangar door and goes inside his apartment for lunch.

Around two o'clock Marty looks outside and sees that the ceilings have raised some. He checks with the weather service and learns that the clouds are hovering at about one thousand feet above the ground. That is not high enough to allow flight away from the airport, but it is high enough for Marty to fly around the pattern a little. He fires up his plane and taxies out again. He taxies to the south end of the runway, and takes off to the north. Marty has more than a mile of visibility. As long as he stays clear of clouds, he can fly in the pattern. He is flying well below the established traffic pattern altitude, but there is no one else here and he is announcing his activities. On his first two landings, Marty lands with some power executing what is known a soft field landing. He does long extended touch-and-goes further packing the snow on the runway.

No special endorsement is needed to fly on skis, but Marty attended a three-day training in Alaska last year, and he is putting his training to use.

On the third landing he does a normal power off landing with no problems. He completes three more power off landings and taxies back to the hangar. Marty has had a great day of flying. He hopes the skies will clear tomorrow.

CHAPTER 13

Turkeyneck spends Sunday night sitting in a recliner looking out onto the airport. All night long he watches as snow falls. He eats snacks from an honor snack bar in the lounge, being very careful to hide his tracks. He plans on hijacking whoever arrives at the airport and making the pilot fly him to Mexico.

In the meanwhile, though, he even has a television to watch.

At ten o'clock, he watches the news. The top story is the weather. Almost the entire state has been shut down by the biggest snow storm in state history. Major roads are being cleared as quickly as possible. Most airports, even in the major cities, are closed. Finally, there are a few words about the robbery. There was an attempted robbery in a local convenience store yesterday. The clerk was wounded, but is expected to live. It is believed that one of the suspects was wounded, but the police have no descriptions. Anyone having any information should contact the police. Things are looking up.

Turkeyneck is comfortable and warm. The airport is completely covered in snow, and no one comes in all day long on Monday. Turkeyneck's plan is to hide in the women's bathroom if he hears anyone come in the building, but that plan faces no test for the entire day.

He has managed to find a VFR sectional map downstairs. He has been studying the map all day, and has actually learned some of the symbols on the map. He has a general idea of the route he will force whoever he hijacks to fly, and has even identified some potential refueling locations.

* * * *

Katie and Bill spend the afternoon playing Casino and watching television in the pilot's lounge at the FBO where they spent the night. Food for the day consists of chips and candy from vending machines.

* * * *

Marty watches television, and then spends the afternoon reading a novel. He has a spinach salad for lunch and tilapia with sautéed mushrooms and peppers over rice for dinner.

* * * *

Carla and John Delgado call Rebecca's parents. Both sets of grandparents agree to tell Rachel nothing right now. The snow has not got as far south as Abilene, and Victoria Long and other members of the Delgado's house church bring meals and prayers throughout the day.

* * * *

Joe and I feed our little fire and chat throughout the afternoon. Even with the fire, the cold is painful. I can tell that Joe is starting to feel the effects. I put his sleeping bag inside mine, and have him spend the day wrapped in two thermal blankets and two sleeping bags. We eat energy bars and drink water.

Night time comes and everyone settles down for another night of restless sleep.

* * * *

Katie and Bill reclaim their respective couches in the pilots' lounge.

* * * *

Carla and John hold each other through the night. Their bedtime prayer is a prayer of thanksgiving for God's divine protection of their son. Carla adds to the prayer: "Lord, my son is a good man. He is a good father. But, Lord, his heart has become so hard since Rebecca went to be with you. It hurts me to see him hurt all the time. Please, Lord, help my son, not just physically but emotionally as well. I ask you not only to bring him through whatever he is going through physically tonight, but to heal his heart too. We pray in the name of your precious son for the recovery of our precious son. Amen."

* * * *

Joe sleeps fitfully. I sit up watching him and the fire. Around midnight I remember that there are two lawn chairs buried in the snow. I dig one out and bring it into the tent. I sit up through the night thinking.

I'm singing softly to myself, making up a ditty of a song.

Cain killed Able.
This I know,
For the Bible tells me so.
Why's that in the Bible, Joe?
What did God want me to know?
Why? Why? Why? Why?
Why's that in the Bible, Joe?
What did God want me to know?

Jonah was a tasty dish
in the belly of a fish.
Why's that in the Bible, Joe?
What did God want me to know?
Why? Why? Why? Why?
Why's that in the Bible, Joe?
What did God want me to know?

Noah built a big old boat.
Didn't know if it would float.
Why's that in the Bible, Joe?
What did God want me to know?
Why? Why? Why? Why?
Why's that in the Bible, Joe?
What did God want me to know?

I wonder. Cain killed Able. He was a murderer, just as surely as the kid who killed my Rebecca. Murderers deserve to die. They don't deserve to live. God should have struck Cain down with a bolt of lightning. I hate the boy who killed Rebecca. God should hate Cain. Why did God simply banish Cain to another country? It's not right. There is no figuring God.

* * * *

I remember. I remember waking up in a hospital with no recollection of where I was. Mom and Dad were there. Joe was there too. They told me there had been an accident. A kid, an eleven year old kid, had stolen a car and was running from the police. I was driving down Lewis Avenue in Tulsa on my way home from church. I never saw the car that hit us. I don't think Rebecca did either. He was going faster than eighty miles an hour when he broadsided us, hitting our car directly on Rebecca's door. Everyone assures me that Rebecca died instantly, that she didn't suffer. I want to know about the kid who killed her. Is he at least dead, or better yet, crippled for life? No. He was not even hurt.

I don't remember the accident at all, even though I was not hurt. Thankfully, Rachel wasn't hurt either. She was in her car seat behind me. Why can't I remember if I wasn't hurt? They tell me I was in shock.

Yes, I was in shock. I'm still in shock all these years later. The stupid punk who killed my wife, who killed the mother of my baby, wasn't even hurt. Did the State at least execute him for what he did? No! He spent two years in a reform school. How could that be? How could God let that happen? What kind of a God lets a sweet person like Rebecca be killed by a punk like the one who killed her? What kind of a God let's a murderer go free, while a precious little girl grows up without her mother? I know what kind of a God can do that: the same kind of God who can simply banish Cain for killing his brother.

A God who can tell Jonah to go to Nineveh, devise an elaborate plan to have a fish eat him, and then forgive his disobedience by having the fish spit him on the shores of the very place He told him to go, is the kind of God who can overlook a punk killing my Rebecca.

What kind of God kills almost every living creature on earth with a flood, and then lets the punk who killed my Rebecca go free?

I don't need that kind of God.

* * * *

I look at Joe. I can tell he is cold and he is in pain. For the first time I begin to think he might not make it through tomorrow. He is shivering. I don't know what to do, so I put more wood on the fire. I look up. I can see stars. The sky has cleared. I think to myself: "We have got to be found tomorrow. Joe won't last another night."

There is a moon out tonight. It is a bright night. I think about Joe's plan to carve an SOS into the snow. We just don't have any tools. Then I think of something. I go outside in the snow taking my lawn chair with me. I fold it up and then lay the back of the chair flat against the snow. I walk backward dragging the chair like a plow through the snow. I travel about ten feet. Then, I turn around and repeat the process going the other way. Before long I have carved a straight line about twenty inches wide by a foot deep by ten feet long. I work through the night dragging the chair back and forth through the snow, and by sunrise I have a clearly discernable SOS carved in the snow in letters ten feet wide and ten feet long. I don't know how good the white on white letters will look from the sky, but I feel like I've accomplished something.

I return to the tent and wait for Joe to wake up. As I watch him sleep, I can tell he is in a bad way.

Even though I have managed to keep a fire going all night long, the fire just hasn't produced enough heat in the tent to keep Joe warm. I decide to dig the other chair out of the snow and set it up near the fire. Joe is stiff now, and cannot get up without my help. Still in the two sleeping bags, I carry him to the chair and set him in it. It is much warmer here. Joe can now see my night's handiwork. He smiles his approval.

For the first time in a long time, I pray: "Lord, please help Joe through this day. Help those who are searching for us. Watch over them, protect them, and lead them to us quickly and safely."

* * * *

At first light on Tuesday, Turkeyneck is awakened from the comfort of his recliner looking out over the runway by a flurry of activity outside. Several city trucks are outside clearing the runway, taxiways and the area leading up to the FBO and gas pumps.

It looks like Shawnee Airport will be open for business today.

CHAPTER 14

The Redcap mission has been approved. Katie will be sitting in the left seat. Her job is to fly the plane. Bill will be in the front right seat. The position is called Observer, but he will be a co-pilot for all practical purposes. Lana Wilson lives near the airport. She has been selected to fill the Scanner position in the left rear seat. Although she is certainly qualified to fill the Scanner position, or any of the other positions in the plane for that matter, Lana gets this assignment because she has the best chance of making it to the airport on the still treacherous city streets.

Tulsa International Airport in some respects operates like two airports using one control tower. Running north-south, the two primary runways are parallel to each other. The control tower is between them. The east runway is longer and wider and primarily serves commercial jet traffic. The west runway is a little shorter and a little narrower. Both runways are capable of handling large jets, but the west runway mostly serves the general aviation population.

While the east runway was re-opened to commercial traffic yesterday, its counterpart to the west is still covered in snow, as are most of the taxiways and parking areas serving the general aviation side of the airport. In anticipation of the search and rescue mission anticipated for today though, airport crews worked through the night to clear a path for the Civil Air Patrol plane to access the east runway.

In an effort to make good use of their time, Katie and Bill are planning their search while they are waiting for Lana. They have been authorized to conduct two consecutive search patterns. Neither of them can remember such authorization having ever been given before. The authorization reflects the realities of the dangerous weather conditions being experienced by any survivors as well as the limited resources available to CAP at the moment. In the entire state, Katie, Bill and Lana represent the only mission ready crew. By this afternoon, a crew should be able to get out of Lawton, but for right now Katie, Bill and Lana represent CAP for the entire state of Oklahoma.

The first mission that has been authorized is a low level route search. Katie will fly to Pogue Airport, about five minutes from Tulsa International. Once there she will establish the plane at approximately one thousand feet above ground level, and trim for flight at ninety miles per hour with ten degrees of flaps. Using flaps in a search does two things. First, it allows a pilot to fly more slowly than he or she otherwise would be able to. Next, it forces the pilot to change the attitude of the plane with a little more nose down attitude. This second feature of the use of flaps improves visibility for the searchers. For safety reasons, CAP regulations prohibit flying at less than one thousand feet above the ground during searches.

Once established at the proper speed and altitude, Katie will fly directly to and over the Shawnee airport. Katie will not be searching for anything. She will fly the plane. Bill will be responsible for the radios and for visually searching the area to the right of the plane. From her position in the back seat, Lana will act as secretary for the mission, keeping track of time in the air, making sure the crew reports back to mission base as required, and helping to monitor fuel consumption. She will also be responsible for searching the area on the left side of the plane.

If the route search fails to produce any sightings by the time the CAP plane reaches Shawnee, Katie will turn the plane around and fly all the way back to Pogue repeating the process in reverse. This second pass over the route puts different eyes on each side of the plane and increases the likelihood of success dramatically. However, if the mission is unsuccessful on this pass, Katie will fly to a pre-selected point twenty miles northeast of Shawnee, and begin the second search using an expanding square search technique.

At 8:00 a.m. sharp, Lana Wilson comes bounding up the stairs of the FBO.

Bill and Katie hear her thundering voice before they see her. "Man I hate snow! I don't just dislike snow, I hate it. Whoever came up with the idea of snow needs to be fired. I didn't move to Oklahoma to be in this kind of snow. If I wanted this kind of snow, I would have stayed in Chicago! This is ridiculous!"

In stark contrast to Bill and Katie who are wearing green military looking flight suits with rank insignia on them, Lana is wearing gray slacks, a blue golf shirt with CAP insignia, a leather bomber jacket, and Ray Ban pilot's sunglasses. She is a beautiful African American woman, standing a full six feet tall with a smile that fills her entire face.

On making eye contact with Katie, she says: "Let's get this show on the road. Let's get these poor people out of the snow and get home. I've got things to do. Man, I hate this snow!"

Katie is putting the finishing touches on her paperwork. She is at a laptop inputting data into the weight and balance spreadsheet. She asks Lana: "Lana, what do you weigh?"

"What do I weigh? Is that what you asked me? Not how do you do, Lana? How have you been Lana? What's going on with you, Lana? No, you jump straight to: 'Lana, what do you weigh?' Well I'll tell you what I weigh. I weigh the same as I did the last time you asked me, and the time before that. I weigh one hundred and ninety-five pounds. That's what I weigh, and if that's a problem, you should have thought about it before you let me drive in this snow, because I'm going on this airplane ride. So, you just type whatever number in that computer that works, because I'm here now. Man I hate this snow!"

Then, Lana smiles that big beautiful smile of hers, and Katie laughs.

"One ninety-five is fine, Lana. You know I have to ask."

* * * *

At that very moment Marty is preparing to land his Piper Super Cub at Pogue. He needs gas. The FBO operator, Ace Stearman, lives at the airport, and is inside the FBO taking care of paperwork. He does not expect any traffic at the airport today. There are almost two feet of snow on the runway.

Over the office radio speaker he hears: "Pogue, Piper 7777 is entering a downwind for a touch and go on Runway Three Five, Pogue."

Recognizing both the pilot's voice and his tail number, Ace walks to a counter and picks up a microphone. "Marty, have you looked at the runway?"

"Yes, Ace, but I didn't expect you to be in. I just thought I'd use the self-service pumps. The pumps are working aren't they?"

"They're working, Marty, but unless you've got skis on that Cub, I wouldn't recommend trying to land here."

Marty doesn't answer. He simply announces the base leg of his approach.

By the time Marty is entering the final leg of his approach to landing, Ace is watching him with binoculars. "Well, I'll be," he says to himself, "he does have skis on that thing."

As Ace watches, Marty does four consecutive touch and go landings packing the snow on the runway. His fifth landing is a full stop landing, but he doesn't actually stop, he keeps the plane in constant motion until it is parked in front of the gas pumps at the FBO.

Ace walks out to greet Marty. They know each other well. Like many pilots in the area, Marty buys his gas at Pogue. It is usually the cheapest gas around. Ace works hard when buying gas to buy when prices are down, and he passes those savings on to his customers.

After some small talk, Ace asks Marty if he has heard about the missing plane. He has not.

"I don't know if you know him or not, but Tom Delgado keeps his Cherokee here at Pogue."

"Sure, I know Tom. Is that who is missing?"

"Yes, Marty, it looks like he went down somewhere between Shawnee and here on Sunday."

"Is anyone looking for him?" Mary asks. Then he remembers something. "You know, Ace, I heard Bill Decker on the radio on Sunday night. He was flying a CAP plane out in the direction of Shawnee. I wonder if that had anything to do with Tom."

"I don't know," replies Ace, "but I hope they find him."

With that Marty says goodbye, and climbs back in his plane, thinking to himself, "Maybe I'll just fly down to Shawnee and back and see what I can see."

*   *   *

Meanwhile, Katie has just asked for clearance to taxi at Tulsa International. Although she has been given detailed instructions on which taxiways to follow, the reality is that she will follow the path that has been cleared specifically for her. A major airport in many ways is like a small city. Runways are lined with businesses, each having access to the runways. Today, in Tulsa, though, only one business on the general aviation side of the airport has runway access. The path that has been cleared from the hangar used by CAP to the east runway exists solely for the purpose of facilitating Katie's Redcap mission.

Even with her own private roadway though, Katie soon finds herself facing an interesting dilemma. She has been cleared to proceed to Runway Three Six Right. To get there, though, she has to cross over the west runway. A pilot who has been cleared to a particular runway has not been cleared to cross intersecting runways. As Katie approaches the crossing point over the west runway, she sees that her path has been pre-cut across the runway, which to either side of her path is almost two feet deep in snow. She stops short of the runway, and asks for permission to cross. An amused air traffic controller, asks her to stand by for a moment while he checks to make sure there is no traffic on the runway. After a suitably dramatic pause, the controller announces that the runway appears to be clear, and authorizes Katie to cross the runway and proceed on to her assigned runway.

At her assigned runway, Katie completes her run-ups and announces to ATC that she is ready for departure. She is instructed to hold short of the runway to wait for other departing traffic. Katie waits to enter Runway Three Six Right from the east, while a large commercial jet enters from the west. The jet pilot recognizes the CAP markings on Katie's Cessna 172, and he knows what her mission is. As the jet enters the runway, the pilot speaks to Katie: "God Speed CAP Thirty Five."

The jet lumbers down the runway on its takeoff roll. Katie is instructed to take Runway Three Six Right for departure, "No Delay."

"No Delay," tells Katie that there is another plane on final for landing on the same runway. She enters the runway and turns left pushing the throttle all the way in. As she does so, she is thinking to herself: "Take off before his take off spot, and climb above his climb path."

Katie does not often have to share runways with large jet aircraft, and doing so presents very real dangers to her. The wake turbulence caused by the jet is sufficient to destroy her plane. She must avoid that wake turbulence. To do so she must get airborne as quickly as possible and stay above the path of the jet that has just departed. She reaches over to her electric flap switch and deploys ten degrees of flaps. Her plane jumps into the cold winter air. As it does so, Katie says: "Thank you, Lord for the gift of flight, and another day to fly."

From the back seat, Katie hears: "Yes, Lord, and Lord Jesus, guide us now in our mission of mercy."

It is 8:35 a.m. Lana logs the time. Then she notes: "fuel: 4.5 hours."

The air traffic controller knows that Katie is dealing with the threat of wake turbulence, and almost immediately clears her to turn on course for Pogue, allowing her to get out of the path of the recently departed jet.

Less than five minutes later, ATC releases Katie, but as the controller is doing so, he advises her to be on the lookout for unidentified traffic that has just departed Pogue. Katie advises that she is "looking for traffic," as she sets her transponder for unmonitored VFR flight and dials in the Pogue radio frequency. All three occupants of the Cessna look around the plane at each other, and then Lana speaks. "Who could possibly be departing Pogue right now."

Katie keys her microphone and announces: "Pogue traffic, CAP Thirty Five has just departed KTUL, and is en route to Pogue. We will be flying at 1,000 feet AGL on a heading of 240 out of Pogue."

Marty hears the announcement, and responds: "CAP Thirty Five, Piper 7777 has just departed Pogue to the north. I have you in sight, and should not be a factor for you."

Katie responds: "Thank you, Piper 7777. May I ask what you are flying?"

"I'm flying a Super Cub with skis."

"Very good," says Katie.

At this point, Bill takes over the radio duties, and says hello to Marty.

"Yes." He confirms they will be flying toward Shawnee. Bill doesn't mind Marty knowing what they are doing, but he doesn't want to say anything that will draw undue attention to his mission. You never know who might be listening.

Marty asks: "Bill, can you leave one radio tuned to this frequency?"

"Sure," answers Bill.

Marty turns his plane around to the southwest, climbing to three thousand five hundred feet. In a few minutes he spots the CAP aircraft flying below him. He slows down to match its speed. Because each plane is a high wing airplane, the Cessna is completely visible to him while he remains completely invisible to the Cessna. Marty is not sure why he is doing what he is doing. He simply feels that he must. He will not interfere with the Cessna's mission, but he will keep it in sight.

CHAPTER 15

Katie announces to her crew that they have entered the search area. Lana makes a notation of the time. Bill makes an announcement on a radio dedicated to the purpose. His message is picked up by a repeater, and relayed to the Incident Commander in Oklahoma City.

At ninety miles per hour, the flight to Shawnee will take about an hour. Bill is looking outside the plane, scanning the ground in a precise pattern. Lana is doing the same from the rear of the plane. She has removed her sun glasses. Glare is a good thing in a search. She wants to be able to see glare.

The search begins immediately. The searchers know that many planes go down within sight of an airport. The work of searching is demanding. There is no chit chat.

Twenty minutes into the flight, Bill thinks he sees something off to the right. Katie flies in that direction, and then circles slowly around what Bill sees. It is nothing, just an old abandoned school bus sitting in a pasture.

114

Katie returns to the original path and proceeds on toward Shawnee.

Thirty minutes into the search, Lana announces the time, and Bill radios to the Incident Commander that everything is going well.

Katie can feel her own restlessness, and senses Bill's and Lana's. She turns ninety degrees to the left, and announces. "We are out of the search area. Everyone take a break." All eyes rest. Bill and Lana reposition themselves in their seats.

Bill asks Katie, "Would you like me to fly for a minute?"

"That's not a bad idea," she says.

"Then, I have the plane," says Bill.

Katie responds: "You have the plane."

Bill repeats: "I have the plane."

Katie closes her eyes and sits back in her seat, while Bill turns the plane through two shallow three hundred and sixty degree turns.

Katie sits back up and announces: "I have the plane."

Bill responds: "You have the plane."

Katie replies: "I have the plane."

Using her GPS to guide her, Katie flies back to the point where she left the search area and re-enters the search path.

Bill and Lana resume their search.

Thirty minutes later, the plane is flying over the Shawnee airport. They have found nothing.

Once again Katie leaves the search area, and allows Bill to fly the plane for a few minutes while she rests. Then, Katie reclaims control of the plane. Lana notes the time. Bill reports in to the Incident Commander. They resume their search moving back over the same territory in the opposite direction.

After thirty minutes, Katie again turns to the right and gives everyone a break.

Another thirty minutes later, they are back over Pogue. Again, they have seen nothing.

For the fourth time, they rest in flight. For the fourth time Lana notes the time. And, for the fourth time, Bill reports in to the Incident Commander.

Now Katie asks Bill to enter the coordinates for the beginning of their second search into the GPS. He does so and they move toward a location, twenty miles northeast of Shawnee. The flaps come out and thy climb to a safer altitude.

They never suspect that Marty is shadowing them, and has been all along.

Twenty miles northeast of Shawnee, Katie descends back down to one thousand feet above the ground, puts ten degrees of flaps in and announces that they are in the search area.

They are now over the area where the plane last reported its position. Katie will fly an expanding square pattern. She flies east for one mile. Then, she flies north for one mile. Then she flies west for two miles. Then she flies south for two miles, turns east and begins the pattern again. She continues this pattern until each leg of flight is twenty miles long. Again, they find nothing.

Katie calls off the search. Lana announces that they must now get fuel. Katie turns toward Shawnee. The plane is roughly at pattern altitude for Shawnee, so Katie does not climb out of the search area. She does take out the flaps and increase her speed.

As she passes over an area that they have been searching unsuccessfully for four hours, she hears Lana exclaim: "Sweet Jesus, I see them. They've even got a giant SOS sign in the snow. How could I have missed that? We've been over this area at least four times"

Bill answers: "It's just a matter of angles, lights and shadows. Thank God we passed over at this angle and at this moment of the day."

CHAPTER 16

Sitting near the fire, Joe is starting to show some color, but he still doesn't look all that good. We have made breakfast out of an energy bar and water. After breakfast, I help Joe go out behind the tent, and steady him from the rear as he takes care of his morning business. Then, I carry him back to his chair, and help him back into his two sleeping bags and back into the lawn chair by the fire. He is exhausted. There is no resemblance between the man who matched me step for step in our fight against the falling snow and the man now sitting in the lawn chair by the fire.

I have brought my lawn chair out by the fire too. We are sitting. We are not talking much. Around 9:00 we hear an airplane. Looking to the north we see a high wing airplane flying very slowly and very low toward us. I run out into the open field which served as our landing strip waving one of the aluminum blankets and screaming at the top of my lungs. The plane is about a mile west of us. When the plane is just about even with our location, it turns sharply to the left, seemingly flying directly to us.

It is not alone. Flying above the plane and behind it is another plane. That seems like a strange way to search but I figure the more eyes the better.

The planes are almost directly over us. I can see that the lower plane has ten degrees of flaps deployed. That tells me that it is intentionally flying slowly. It is certainly looking for us.

Almost directly overhead, the plane makes a shallow three hundred sixty degree circle to the left. Instinctively I time the circle. It takes two minutes. That is a standard rate turn. They must be telling us that they see us. The plane makes another standard rate turn full circle to the left. The higher flying airplane copies the movements of the lower. Then, both planes fly directly back to the position where they turned off of the original course and re–enter that course. The lower plane is still searching. The higher appears to be following the lower.

I am puzzled. If the searchers had seen us, there would be no reason for them to maintain a search attitude, configuration and speed. If they needed gas, for example, they could lock our position into their GPS unit, and then fly on to their destination. They would not need to continue flying so low or so slowly. It is obvious that they are still searching. They did not see us. How could they not have seen us? My heart is sinking.

Joe says: "Cheer up, Thomas. They'll be back. I told you, I still have some business to attend to."

I don't respond. I look at Joe, and think to myself: "I'm not sure, Joe."

An hour passes, and then, we hear two planes coming back toward us from the southwest. It appears to be the same pair retracing their route. They are flying our route! They are still looking for us. Again, I run to the field waving the aluminum blanket and screaming. Again, the planes near our position and turn abruptly to the left. They fly away for about a mile, and then do two standard rate turns to the left again.

The planes returns to the original path, turn left again, and fly slowly off to the northeast, apparently still searching for us.

They did not see us. I look at Joe. He won't make it through another night. I've got to do something. I am thinking about walking out to get help. What should I do with Joe? Will he be safer in the tent or by the fire? I'll have to put him back in the tent. I don't know how long I'll be gone, and I don't know how long the fire will last. I'll let Joe warm up for another hour. Then I'll put him in the tent and start walking.

Almost on the hour, I hear the planes returning from the northeast. They are coming back. They are not low and slow this time. They are flying with a purpose. Both planes pass over our position until they are just out of sight, but we can still hear them. They cut power. What are they doing?

After several minutes Joe catches sight of both planes. We watch as the planes fly a distance of about two miles from the south to the north. They turn to the west and fly about the same distance. They are in the same configuration as before. One is high. One is low. When they have flown about two miles to the west, they turn back to the south, and then out of sight. They are flying an expanding spiral. They will be coming back. They will be flying directly over us.

Over what seems to be an eternity we watch the planes search to the south of us, to the east of us, directly over us, to the west of us, then full circle again until they are searching north of us. They have missed us again, but they keep flying by. Each time they go by, their path gets longer, and the time between sightings gets greater.

Finally, we see both planes approaching from the west. They are much faster now. They are abandoning the search.

I sit in my chair, dejected. I have wasted precious time watching these planes fly in circles. They are directly overhead now, and they are too fast to be searching, but the lower flying plane makes a steep turn to the left. As it flies back over our position, the plane rocks its wings dramatically.

We have been found! We are going home.

CHAPTER 17

Katie is thrilled beyond words. Not only have they found the people they are looking for, at least one of them appears to be alive and mobile.

"Oh Lord, thank you, thank you, thank you," she says to herself.

She gets a chorus of "Amens" from Bill and Lana.

Then, over their headphones the trio hears: "Bill, do you still have 122.7 turned on?"

They look around the cabin at each other as if they've just heard from God. Everyone smiles in amusement, and then Bill keys his mike and responds: "Yes, Marty I still have this frequency dialed in."

Before Bill can tell Marty the good news, Marty says: "Well it looks like you've found something. Can I be of any assistance?"

"Where are you, Marty?"

"About a half mile behind you, and a couple of thousand feet up."

Katie shivers, and says over the intercom to Bill and Lana: "Has he been following us all morning long? That's creepy."

123

Bill asks Marty: "Have you been following us?"

There is a long pause as Marty tries to think of an answer. After a full thirty second delay, he comes up with just the right answer.

"Yes."

"Why?" asks Bill.

"I'm not sure, Bill, but looking at the terrain, it might be good that I did. Do you mind if I drop down and take a look? I may be able to land on the snow and get these people out of there."

All three in the CAP plane know that they are completely breaking protocol simply by talking with Marty, but it is Lana who finally suggests what should be obvious.

"You know," she says over the intercom "We don't have a ground team we can send in after these people, and he does have skis on that plane. I believe him when he says he doesn't know why he followed us, but I don't believe it was any accident. He's supposed to be here, and we had best just get out of his way."

Katie offers: "Well we can't authorize him to do anything, but we don't have any authority to prohibit him from doing anything either. Why don't you tell him that, Bill?"

Bill keys the mike and says: "Marty I don't have the authority to confirm or deny what you are asking. Neither do I have the authority to tell you where you can or can't fly or land. We are going to climb up to about three thousand feet AGL, and circle this site as long as we can. We will report our status to our Incident Commander. I will also keep this frequency open."

Marty responds: "I understand."

With that Marty begins his descent to what he perceives to be one thousand feet above ground level. He makes two slow passes over the site of the suspected plane crash, and determines that the field is suitable for landing. He announces his intentions on 122.7 just as if he were making an approach at an airport.

"Piper 7777 is entering a downwind for landing in a field twenty miles northeast of Shawnee. I will be landing to the north."

Then, a moment later he announces: "Piper 7777 is entering base for a landing in a field twenty miles northeast of Shawnee, landing to the north."

And finally, he announces: "Piper 7777 is entering final for a landing in a field twenty miles northeast of Shawnee. This will be a touch and go, landing to the north. I need to pack this snow a little before I make a full stop landing."

Marty repeats this entire process three times.

Meanwhile, Bill is communicating with the Incident Commander, giving as many particulars as he can. People are thrilled with the apparent success of the mission, but perplexed to know there is a ski plane so close by, and wonder why the plane is landing.

* * * *

Joe and I are ecstatic. We see the plane that first spotted us begin to climb, while the second plane is descending. Joe is still in his chair, but he is looking skyward. He comments: "That is a Super Cub on skis."

"Well what do you know about that?" I ask.

"It looks like we're going to get rescued by a real pilot with some tail dragger time," says Joe.

As we watch the Super Cub fly a rectangular landing pattern, Joe observes: "perfect school boy pattern. I like this guy."

Finally, the plane is on short final touching down on the far end of the pasture but coming toward us. The pilot doesn't land though. He performs a touch and go. I am puzzled and concerned.

Again, it is Joe who figures things out. "He's packing the snow. He'll do one or two more passes before he lands. Thomas, before he gets here, there is something I want to talk to you about."

"Sure, Joe. What's on your mind?"

"That's a two place plane, and he's going to have to take us out of here one at a time. Of course, I'll go first, because I'm not doing very well. I know that. Before I go, though, I want you to think about something. You mean the world to me, Thomas. I only knew you a month before Rebecca went on to be with the Lord, but that was long enough to know that you've changed. You've changed a great deal, and not really for the better. It hurts me to see the hatred you carry around with you, and my friend, it is hurting you too.

I want you to know something else, Thomas. I know that today has been and is going to be a landmark day in your life. This day is a long way from over. Big things are going to happen today. Please promise me that you will give God a chance today."

I am afraid that my friend Joe is losing it. I simply consent to his request.

* * * *

We watch intently as the Super Cub makes a full stop landing and taxies in our direction. The pilot is working hard to keep the tail wheel out of the snow. He is kicking up a cloud of snow as he travels across the pasture.

When he is about a hundred yards from us, the pilot lets the tail of the plane drop, and it seems to act like a brake. The plane comes to a full stop about forty feet from us, and I wade out to meet the pilot.

Even before the pilot emerges from the plane, I recognize the plane. It is Marty Dixon's Super Cub. I have never seen it on skis before, but I recognize the plane. Sure enough, it is Marty who climbs out of the plane, carrying what appears to be a thermos bottle, and steps into the snow. He sinks down to about knee level, and works his way in my direction. We don't know each other well, but are able to greet each other by name.

Marty says: "How are you, Tom?"

I reply: "I've seldom been better than right now Marty, but I've got Joe Eastman with me, and I think we need to get him out of here pretty soon. We are walking back toward Joe as we talk.

"I don't think I know Joe," says Marty.

"He's an older fellow, Marty. He flies with me a lot. You've probably seen him with me at Enrique's in Ponca City or at one of the local fly-ins." Enrique's is a Mexican Restaurant located on the runway at the Ponca City airport about fifty miles from Sand Springs. It is a favorite of pilots from all over the state of Oklahoma.

By now Marty can see Joe, and he responds: "Oh, sure, I recognize him. Is he hurt?"

"He's tired and cold, Marty. We made a hard landing, and the plane burned up, but neither of us was hurt in the landing."

Now, we have reached Joe, and I introduce Marty to him.

"Marty Dixon, I'd like you to meet my good friend, Joe Eastman."

Joe doesn't wait for Marty to say anything. He extends his hand in friendship and says: "It is a great honor and pleasure to meet you, Martin." I pick up on Joe's use of the formal name, and smile inwardly. I know that Joe always uses people's proper names, but I've never asked him why. That's just the way Joe is.

"Are you going to take me for a ride?" Joe asks Marty.

"That's the plan, Joe. Can I offer you some coffee first?"

"I thought you'd never ask," says Joe.

At that, Marty pours Joe some coffee from the thermos. The effect when Joe takes a sip is immediate and miraculous. All the color returns to his face, and he stops shivering.

"Are you up to a little trip?" Marty asks Joe.

"Yes, I am, and by the way I'm glad they sent a real pilot who knows how to fly a tail dragger."

"Do you drive tail draggers?" asks Marty.

"Yes, I own a Luscombe. I flew it all the way to Canada and back once, using no navigation equipment except a compass. I took my wife along with me, of course. Someone had to prop the engine."

I've heard this story at least a hundred times, but I laugh anyway. I laugh because I knew it was coming the second Marty asked Joe if he had ever flown a tail dragger.

"Well," says Marty, "We'd better get a move on."

With that I lift Joe out of the chair. Marty gets behind me and steadies me as we walk toward his plane. The walk is very tough in the knee-deep snow.

At the plane, Marty helps me put Joe in the rear seat and buckle him in. Marty makes a move toward the front seat, and Joe says: "Not so fast, Martin. Where's my headset?"

Marty is about to protest that Joe won't really need a headset for the short ride he'll be taking to Shawnee, but I give him a look that says: "Don't bother. Just give him a headset."

Marty looks in a pilot bag which is stowed behind Joe, and produces a headset. He plugs it in, and hands the headset to Joe. Joe puts the headset on and says: "Okay, I'm ready now."

With that, Marty climbs into the front seat and I move away from the plane.

Marty starts the engine. It appears that he needs a great deal of power to start the plane moving. Once it is moving though, he backs off the power and makes a wide right turn back to the south. At the far end of the pasture, he makes another wide right turn back in my direction, puts in power and takes off. It is a beautiful sight.

I gather my survival kit and sit down by the fire to wait for my ride to safety.

* * * *

As the plane lifts off, Joe says: "Thank you, Lord for the gift of flight and another day to fly."

Marty thinks to himself that he is a little surprised that Joe is not afraid of flying after what he has been through.

Then, he hears: "Martin?"

"Yes, Joe, and by the way, you don't have to call me Martin, Marty will do."

"There's a reason you are named Martin. You should use your name. Just think about that. Anyway, Martin, thank you for coming to get me."

"You're welcome."

"I was expecting you. Today is going to be a very special day for you."

"It has already been pretty special, Joe."

"It's going to get more special, Martin. You are going to see three trees planted in the Lord's orchard. There will be room for a fourth. I will be praying that that tree gets planted too. This is a special time in God's calendar. It is a time for planting trees. Old trees will be making way for the new. I am praying for four new trees, so please pay attention today."

Marty thinks to himself, "The old man is worse off than I thought."

Marty radios ahead to Shawnee that he is inbound, and in need of an ambulance.

When he gets to Shawnee, he finds the runway cleared of snow. He will have to land parallel to the runway. He announces his intentions and lands on the snow, turns around and taxies on the snow around the end of the runway and to the gas pumps. The snow has not been cleared north of the gas pumps, and he is able to taxi close enough to get fuel.

Marty carries Joe into the FBO to await the ambulance, and returns to his plane.

He takes off on his way back to the crash site.

*   *   *   *

All the while, Turkeyneck watches from upstairs in the FBO. He wants to make his move, and hijack Marty, but he has no clear path. He is nervous. He will have to move soon. Things are happening quickly, and Turkeyneck doesn't like it.

*   *   *   *

"Katie, you need to go for fuel, now." Lana's voice is firm.

"Just a few more passes, Lana," says Katie. We'll leave when the Cub gets back."

"Major, knock it off." Even though Katie is a Major and Bill and Lana are both Lieutenants, Lana has just pulled rank on her. Anyone in CAP has the right to call "knock it off" on anyone else in

CAP if they are engaging in dangerous behavior. Lana has just called "knock it off" on Katie, and in doing so, she has brought Katie back to her senses.

Katie immediately turns toward Shawnee. She is low on fuel, and the one unforgiveable sin of a CAP pilot is to run out of gas. Running out of gas means being forever barred from flying a Civil Air Patrol plane. Katie must go get gas.

*   *   *   *

I am alone now. My emotions are taking control. I feel like I might cry, but I don't know why. I'll be home soon, but the emotions I'm feeling are not the emotions I expected to feel. I'll be glad when this day is over, and I am at home asleep in my own bed.

CHAPTER 18

Marty is in his plane preparing to go back to the crash site before Turkeyneck can scramble down the stairs to hijack him. Besides that Joe is downstairs waiting for an ambulance. There is just too much activity right now. Turkeyneck bides his time.

As Joe is sitting in an office chair downstairs, he is being tended to by Chris. Joe's recovery is already very noticeable. He is still very stiff from the physical exertion from two nights ago, but he is communicating well and seems already to be on the mend. Joe catches a glimpse of Turkeyneck upstairs, but it means nothing to him and he says nothing.

The front door to the FBO opens, and two EMTs come in. They check Joe's vitals and chat with him. There is no question as to whether he will be going to the hospital. He will be, but there does not appear to be any need to rush. One of the EMTs is chatting Joe up, while filling out some paperwork. He asks if Joe has any identification, and Joe produces a driver's license from his billfold.

"Wow!" says the EMT who appears to be in his early twenties. "You were born in 1918!"

"That's right," says Joe, "but keep it to yourself."

"But that means you're like ninety years old."

"I'll be ninety three on my next birthday," says Joe, "but like I said, I'd really prefer that you keep that to yourself. If people knew how old I was, they'd start treating me like an old man."

"You are an old man," says the young EMT with a smile on his face. "And, your driver's license is still good. That's amazing. I'm impressed."

The conversation has a good-natured quality about it, and Joe decides to really impress the young EMT.

"That's nothing," he says as he hands the young man a folded piece of card stock from his billfold.

The young man examines the paper, and recognizes it immediately.

"Do you know what that is?" Joe asks.

"I know exactly what this is," says the EMT. "I've got one just like it in my wallet."

"Okay," says the other EMT who has been listening, "I'll bite. What is it?"

"This," says the first EMT, "is a valid third class medical certificate from the FAA, which by way was recently issued and will still be good for almost two years." Turning to Joe, he continues: "You are correct, sir. I am impressed."

Joe just smiles, and asks: "So are you boys taking me somewhere or not?"

The young men help Joe onto their gurney, and proceed out the front door to the waiting ambulance.

* * * *

Marty and Katie pass each other. She is heading in for gas. Marty is on his way to complete the rescue mission.

Marty flies straight in and lands, and I walk out to meet him. He doesn't even get out of the plane. I am carrying my survival kit. There are things in the kit which should not be left out for people to stumble upon.

Almost as quickly as I am strapped in, Marty is taxiing back to his landing spot to take off to the north.

I put on the headset and say hello to Marty.

"Smokey is not going to be very happy with us," he answers.

I left my fire burning.

"Do you really think there is any chance of the fire spreading?" I ask.

"No, I don't," he says.

With that, Marty gives the plane some gas. As we lift off, something unknown, deep inside me causes me to say: "Thank you, Lord for the gift of flight and another day to fly."

Marty hears me on the intercom and says: "Your friend said the same thing."

"He always does. I think that's why I said it."

Marty asks: "Well, where do you want to go? I can take you to Sand Springs or Tulsa. Or, I can take you to Shawnee first, if you'd like to meet the people who found you. They are there now getting gas."

I say: "I'd like to meet the CAP crew, if that's okay."

Marty says: "That's okay. In fact, I've been hoping to meet the pilot myself."

He turns the Super Cub toward Shawnee.

* * * *

As Katie is nearing the airport, the three crew members draw straws to see who gets to run to the bathroom first, while the others supervise the refueling. Katie wins.

As soon as she touches down, she makes a bee line for the bathroom. She has been in the air for four hours.

Bill and Lana tend to the plane and supervise the refueling.

Turkeyneck watches from upstairs.

In a few minutes, the refueling is done. Lana, Bill and the young man working at the airport walk back toward the FBO. Katie meets them about half way. She is on her way back to the plane to complete some paperwork in the cockpit.

Lana and Bill walk straight to the bathrooms on the first floor when they enter the building. The young man who is running the FBO goes into his first floor office. Katie climbs into the cockpit.

Turkeyneck makes his move.

He is down the stairs in a flash and running out the door toward the plane. He runs to the right side of the plane and opens the passenger door. The first thing Katie sees is a gun pointed at her head.

As Turkeyneck climbs in the plane, he orders Katie to: "Get this airplane in the air right now, or I will blow your brains out."

Katie is frightened, but she is cool. She says: "You really don't want to do this."

She hears: "Don't tell me what I do or don't want to do. You do what I tell you to do, and no one gets hurt. You don't get hurt, and your friends in the bathroom don't get hurt. Now, start this plane, and start it now."

Katie says: "I need to follow a check list. This isn't a car. I can't just start it like a car."

Turkeyneck says: "I don't care about your checklist. You can do your checklist after we are in the air. Start the engine now, or I will shoot you."

Katie puts the key in the ignition. She pushes the mixture to rich. She turns her mags on. She yells: "Clear Prop."

She starts the engine. As soon as the engine starts, she reaches up to the instrument panel and turns on her electronics. Then, she punches in 7500 on a panel in front of her. She has just entered the code indicating that her airplane has been hijacked into her transponder. That code will be picked up on Air Traffic Controller's radar, and will allow them to follow her. It will also warn them to be careful about what they say to her on radio.

She has her headset on and she motions for Turkeyneck to put his on. He does so. Katie pushes a button on the instrument panel and switches from the frequency for Shawnee airport to the one for Pogue. She hopes Marty is still tuned in to Pogue.

Katie pushes her microphone button and says: "Sir, you will have to push the button on the yoke in front of you, if you want to talk with me."

Then, before, Turkeyneck can respond she pushes the button again, and announces: "Shawnee Airport, CAP 35 is squawking seven five zero zero, and taxiing to runway Three Five for departure." Now in addition to sending out a "hijack" signal on her transponder,

Katie has just communicated the same information to anyone who might be listening to her radio transmission. She knows there is no control tower at the Shawnee airport. She is hoping that Marty is still tuned into this frequency, and that he will know how to respond.

Turkeyneck pushes his own microphone button, and says: "What's that all about? Who are you talking too? Don't think I won't kill you."

Katie pushes her microphone button again and says: "Just relax sir. If I don't follow certain protocols we will be intercepted by F-16s, and I don't think you want that. I have to get clearance before we take off, that's all."

* * * *

Marty and I hear both sides of this entire conversation. By pushing their microphone buttons, both Katie and Turkeyneck are transmitting on their radio. They are not talking on their intercom like Turkeyneck thinks.

Marty quickly picks up on what is happening. He takes his cue and decides to imitate Air Traffic Control, and let Katie know that he will be with her. He keys his microphone and says: "CAP Thirty-five you are cleared for departure."

"Thank you Shawnee. CAP Thirty-five is taking Runway Three Five for departure. What direction will we be going, Sir?" she asks her captor.

"Go south," says Turkeyneck.

"We will be going South, Shawnee."

Again, Marty answers: "CAP Thirty-five, you are cleared for departure to the south. We have you in sight."

Katie takes off to the north, and starts an immediate turn to the south.

Marty and I are behind her and above her. We are in her blind spot.

Marty and I are talking back and forth quickly. Almost off-handedly he asks me: "I don't guess you have a gun in that survival kit, do you."

I answer, "Yes, I do."

Marty is flipping back and forth on frequencies talking to Flight Service in McAlester, Oklahoma.

* * * *

Lana and Bill walk out onto the tarmac just in time to see their airplane take off. They run inside and try to talk with Katie from a radio in the FBO, but Katie is not listening to the Shawnee frequency. She is afraid someone will say something her captor shouldn't hear.

In a few minutes, though the FBO phone rings. The young man working there answers it, and then asks: "Is one of you Lt. Decker?"

"That's me," says Bill.

Bill takes the phone. It is flight service in McAlester informing him of what has just happened. There is nothing he can do, except make phone calls and wait. That is what he and Lana do. They make phone calls, and they wait.

*　*　*　*

"Stay as low as you can. Stay under the radar." says Turkeyneck.

"That is very dangerous," answers Katie.

Turkeyneck answers in a threatening tone: "I'll tell you what is dangerous. Dangerous is not doing exactly what I tell you to do."

Marty and I listen to every conversation between Katie and her captor.

As she is flying, Katie is thinking. Her Cessna 172 will run off and leave Marty's Super Cub. She used ten degrees of flaps when she took off. She leaves the flaps in, and trims up for an airspeed of eighty five miles per hour. She knows that Marty's plane can fly around one hundred miles per hour with wheels. She does not know how fast it can fly with skis, but she does know that it kept up with her all morning at ninety miles per hour. Eighty-five miles per hour should be fine. She levels off at what she estimates to be one thousand five hundred feet above ground level.

Marty and I are right behind her.

"Do you have a plan?" I ask Marty.

"Right now we just keep her in sight, stay out of sight and listen. Tell me about this gun you have in your survival kit."

CHAPTER 19

Strapped to the outside of my survival kit with Velcro is a canvas bag. Inside the bag is what appears to be nothing more than the stock of a rifle. That is exactly what it is, but inside the rifle stock are the receiver, barrel, and two eight round clips for a Henry .22 caliber survival rifle.

I tell Marty what I have.

He is not satisfied with the fact that the gun is only a .22 caliber rifle.

I reply that it is better than nothing, and that it is all we have, unless he has something in his plane.

He does not have a gun of his own.

Marty asks: "Do you think you could shoot the hijacker if I dropped in close to them on his side of the plane."

I reply: "that's a pretty bad idea, Marty." I might miss and hit Katie. I might hit him and make him mad. I might hit Katie's plane, and cause something horrible to happen. We better just follow them for a while."

* * * *

Janson Parker is heading west on McArthur toward the airport. As he comes out of the tunnel which passes under the runway, he sees a car parked in the parking lot of the Gordon Cooper Tech Center. Even covered in snow, Parker recognizes the car as Turkeyneck Gibson's blue 1978 Monte Carlo. He radios in to headquarters asking to have a patrolman take a look at the car.

When he gets to the airport, Parker is met by Chris, the young man working there, and the two Civil Air Patrol volunteers. They tell him what has happened.

Parker has no procedure to follow. He follows his instincts, and decides that he must notify the Federal Aviation Administration, the Oklahoma Highway Patrol, and the FBI. After gathering as much information as he can, Parker goes to his car to start the communication process.

* * * *

Officer Jim Douglas has been a police officer for less than three months. He is alone when he pulls into the parking lot of the Gordon Cooper Tech Center, and not happy about having to get out in the snow to look at a car which appears to him to be legally parked. He walks up to the driver's window, and clears the snow off the window. Cupping his hands over his eyes, he looks into the window, and with some effort discerns the form of a man lying down in the front seat. Douglas taps on the window, but gets no response. He raps harder, first with his fist, and then with his flashlight. Again, he gets no response.

Douglas returns to his patrol car and attempts to contact Parker. He reports his findings to Parker. Parker asks: "Do you think the person in the car may be in danger?"

"I guess so," says Douglas.

"Then you had better get a look inside. Do you have a slim jim in your car?" A slim jim is a device which will enable Douglas to open the locked car door.

"Yes Sir, I do," replies Douglas.

Without waiting for a response, Douglas returns to the Monte Carlo and in less than a minute pops the lock on the driver's door. He opens the door, and discovers the body of Squat Baker.

Douglas returns to his car and contacts Parker.

"Detective Parker," he says "I think I just solved your convenience store shooting. Squat Baker is in this car, and he's deader than a door nail. I think he's been shot."

Parker tells Douglas to belay the radio traffic and protect the crime scene. With this information, Parker is pretty sure he knows who his hijacker is too.

* * * *

By the time the Oklahoma Highway Patrol dispatches an airplane to look for Katie's plane, she has already crossed the Red River into Texas. Katie tries to engage Turkeyneck in conversation. He agrees to allow her to stop for fuel. She suggests Abilene, and he doesn't object.

Marty and I radio ahead that the plane will be stopping for fuel in Abilene. There will be a welcome party waiting for it when it arrives.

Marty tells me that we have a problem. The Red River seems to be southernmost point of the snow. We have skis on the plane with no place to land. Marty can make it to Abilene, but he cannot make it back to the snow before he runs out of fuel.

"I have no intention of turning back," he says. "Do you have a problem with making another off field landing?"

I'm not thrilled with the idea, but I don't want to turn back either. I tell him so.

"Then we're in for the duration," says Marty.

I agree.

Since there will be a police escort waiting for Katie when we get to Abilene, I decide that I won't be needing my rifle. I have not put it together, and I put it back in its bag.

CHAPTER 20

Abilene is a city of about one hundred thousand people. It has a large well-trained police department. That police department has a SWAT team, and that SWAT team has been alerted and is in position at the Abilene airport.

One member of that team is dressed very casually and is carrying two flashlights with orange cones on the end. He will meet Katie's plane, and direct it to a predetermined point at one of the local FBOs.

Three snipers with assault rifles are hidden at three points within fifty yards of the spot where Katie will park the airplane. When they have their shot, they will take it.

* * * *

As the Cessna is nearing the windmill farm north of Abilene, Turkeyneck asks Katie how far out they are. He does not push the microphone button before he speaks to her. Just as he is about to reach for the button and repeat his question, Katie answers his question.

"We are pretty close," she says. "In fact I will be required to make radio contact with the airport before we can enter their airspace."

The wheels are spinning in Turkeyneck's head. He wonders why Katie has been having him push the microphone button for almost two hours. He concludes that someone is listening to their conversation.

Turkeyneck reaches up the yoke pretending to push the microphone button, and asks Katie: "Who do you have to talk to and why?"

He watches as Katie pushes her microphone button and answers him: "We are approaching Class C airspace. Abilene is a controlled airport. We cannot enter their airspace until we have communicated with the control tower, and we cannot land at the airport without permission from the control tower."

Turkeyneck realizes that Katie is transmitting her plans to someone. That means the police will be waiting for them when they land.

* * * *

"Tom, is it just me, or are we hearing only one side of the conversation between Katie and her hijacker now?"

"It's not just you, Marty. The bad guy is not pushing his microphone button anymore. You had better inform ATC in Abilene."

Marty reports this turn of events to Abilene, but no one has a plan B. They will stick with plan A.

* * * *

"I don't believe you," says Turkeyneck. I don't believe you have to talk with anyone."

Katie asks if she can show him something on a sectional map, and Turkeyneck allows her to pull a map from a map pocket by her left leg. Katie locates the Abilene airport, and shows it to Turkeyneck.

"Do you see those two magenta colored circles around the airport?" she asks.

"Yes."

"Those circles indicate the Abilene airspace. I have to be talking with ATC to enter that airspace."

Turkeyneck is now studying the map. He notices that there appears to be another airport outside the smaller of the two concentric circles Katie has shown him.

He asks: "What's the difference between the outer and the inner circle?"

Katie answers truthfully: "I can go under the outer circle without talking to ATC, but I can't invade the inner circle. It reaches all the way to the ground."

"Then you listen, and you listen carefully, lady. You get under the first circle now."

Katie agrees to descend immediately.

Then Turkeyneck continues: "I don't know how stupid you think I am, but I know that I am not that stupid. I know that we are expected in Abilene. We are not going there. And, I'll tell you something else, if I see your hand move anywhere near that microphone button, again, I will shoot you in the hand. Now pick another airport."

He hands the map back to Katie and she studies it. Finally, in exasperation she reports that they are too low on fuel to go anywhere else.

Turkeyneck grabs the map out of Katie's hand and points to the airport just outside the inner circle. It is Elmdale Airport. "You land there!" he screams. "And, you don't say a word to anyone. Just do it."

"I'm not familiar with that airport," pleads Katie. "I don't even know if they have fuel tanks there."

"For your sake, you better hope they do." Turkeyneck has lost his patience at this point he is yelling at Katie and she is afraid.

Turkeyneck realizes that if Katie had landed at Abilene, he would almost certainly have been shot by a sniper. He wishes he had at least one bullet in his gun, because he really wants to shoot Katie, even if only in the hand.

* * * *

Marty and I watch intently as the Cessna rapidly descends and takes a path to the east of the Abilene Airport.

"What do you think they are doing?" asks Marty.

"I don't know."

Then I realize, Katie is on a short final for a landing at Elmdale airport.

"They are landing at Elmdale!" I yell.

Marty relays this information to Abilene ATC who in turn passes it on the Abilene police department.

"Do you know the airport?" Marty asks.

"Yes! I learned to fly here."

I go on: "Marty there is a grass strip parallel to the runway. Do you think you can land on it?"

"I think so," says Marty. "I'll try anyway."

"Okay," I say, "stay behind them and to the left. They will land on the paved runway, and we will land on the grass. There is a shack of an FBO on the right about half way down the runway. They will have to turn right when they pass the FBO to taxi to the gas pumps. If you are able to get stopped before we reach the FBO, I don't think they will see us. We can sneak around the north side of the FBO through some T hangars and get almost on top of them at the pumps."

"It sounds like we have a plan," says Marty.

Then a horrible thought comes to me. "Marty, we have a problem. The gas pumps here are set up on an honor system. You have to have permission to use the pumps, and you have to know the combination to the padlock on the pumps. There's no way the pilot knows that code."

Marty thinks a moment, and then asks "What is the code?"

I answer: "7743."

Just as the Cessna is about to touch down, Marty keys his microphone and says: "seven seven four three."

CHAPTER 21

Turkeyneck is trying hard to keep his composure, but things are getting out of hand and he knows it. Just as Katie lines up for a landing on Runway One Seven at Elmdale Airport, he and Katie hear a radio transmission: "seven seven four three." Turkeyneck explodes: "What is that? Is that code? What's going on?"

Katie truthfully has no idea, and she tells Turkeyneck so. He doesn't believe her. Frantically, he is looking out the windows of the plane. He sees nothing. He can see for miles in every direction, except for above him and to the rear.

The wheels to the Cessna touch down about a third of the way down the length of the runway, and Katie taxies on to the only runway exit she can see, just south of an old yellow frame building about midway down the length of the runway. She doesn't know where the gas pumps are located, and she can't find them. The airport appears to be completely empty.

As Katie passes the yellow frame building, she turns right and immediately sees two gasoline pumps about a hundred yards ahead of her. She points the pumps out to Turkeyneck, and he strains to look in every direction. There is no sign of life at the airport, and Turkeyneck allows Katie to taxi to the pumps. When she shuts the engine down, he demands the keys from her, and then crawls out of the passenger door dragging her behind him. Once outside the plane, Turkeyneck tightly holds Katie close to his chest in an effort to use her as a shield. He looks in every direction, starting with above them and in the direction from which they just came. He sees nothing that worries him.

* * * *

As soon as Marty sees Katie touch down on the runway, he shuts the engine of the Super Cub off by pulling the mixture control to idle cutoff. He is about a half mile behind Katie lined up with a grass runway running parallel to the runway Katie is landing on. He kills his engine for two reasons. First, he does not want Katie's captor to hear his plane when she shuts hers down. Second, he does not know whether he can successfully land his ski equipped plane on a grass strip. He is preparing for a crash landing.

Marty knows that the situation before him calls for a soft field landing bringing his plane down as slowly as possible with the use of power throughout the landing, but he also knows that he cannot risk the sound of an engine. And, he knows that he must come to a complete stop before he reaches the yellow FBO building halfway down the runway. Not only must he stop, he must stop without the use of brakes. Because his plane is on skis, he has no brakes. On the snow he was able to use his tail wheel as a kind of brake by letting it fall into the snow. He cannot do that on grass.

Marty is thrilled when he sees Katie land almost a third of the way down the runway. That gives him the opportunity to stay behind her. Marty turns off the gas to his engine, and shuts down all electronics. He prepares for a crash. He is only a few feet above the ground when he hears: "Remember, Marty, fly as far into the crash as you can," from the back seat. He knows that I am telling him to fly the plane no matter how rough things get. He must maintain control of the plane throughout the landing or crash, as the case may be.

Marty touches down on the very edge of the grass runway and we hit hard, bouncing once, twice, and then three times. On the third touchdown the Cub sticks to the ground, sliding along the grass at about thirty five miles per hour. Marty is using a great deal of rudder control to keep the tail of the plane from swinging around to the front. We seem to slide forever. As we get slower, the tail wheel drops to the ground, forcing Marty to work the rudder pedals even harder. Finally, though, we come to a complete stop directly across from the yellow FBO. We are invisible to Katie and her captor.

Before we touched down I had removed my rifle from its bag and assembled the receiver to the stock. I am now holding the stock and receiver in my right hand and the barrel in my left. The two eight round clips are in my shirt pocket.

As Marty and I climb out of the plane, I attach the barrel to my rifle, insert one of the clips, and pull back on the safety lever on the right side of the receiver. We run directly to the east side of the yellow FBO, and slowly creep around to the north side. On the north side of the building, we remain shielded from the view of the gas pumps. When I get to the northwest corner of the building, I peek around the corner. I still cannot see the pumps. Behind the FBO is a row of hangars running north to south. Really, they are more hail sheds than hangars, because they are open to the east and west. The end wall on the south side of the hangars blocks my view of the gasoline pumps. We use the wall to shield our approach as we move closer to the pumps. When we reach this wall, we are only about thirty feet from the pumps, and we can hear Katie and her captor talking.

*   *   *   *

Satisfied that they are not under surveillance, Turkeyneck releases his grip on Katie and allows her to open the baggage compartment of the Cessna 172. She removes a small three step ladder which she places near the leading edge of the left wing. As she walks to the gas pumps, Katie sees that the pump is locked with a padlock. She tries to remain calm as she considers various methods different airports use to allow pilots to have easy access to the pumps while, at the same time, preventing strangers from stealing gas. She takes the padlock in her left hand and turns it up. When she does do, she sees that it is a combination lock using four digits. She remembers the last radio transmission she heard before landing: seven seven four three. She tries the combination, and the lock opens. Katie places the pad lock on top of the gas pump.

Turkeyneck suspects nothing. It doesn't even occur to him to wonder how Katie knew the combination.

Katie grounds the airplane with a ground wire from the gas pumps, and climbs up on the ladder to fill the left tank. Turkeyneck is standing next to her with his revolver pointed at her. Glancing at the padlock for the first time, something causes him to walk over to it, pick it up and look at the combination. When Turkeyneck sees the combination seven seven four three displayed on the bottom of the lock, his hear sinks.

Without saying a word, Turkeyneck runs ten feet back to Katie and snatches her off of the ladder, thrusting the revolver in her face. Before he can say a word, though, he finds himself looking down the barrel of my rifle.

CHAPTER 22

Just as I turn to go around the south wall of the hangar that has been hiding Marty and me, Katie's captor is jerking her off of a ladder. I level the rifle and point straight at Katie's captor's head.

Katie appears to be a full foot shorter than her captor. I am thirty feet away from them, and I have a clear shot at the captor's head even though he is holding Katie tight against his chest.

Katie's captor and I make eye contact with each other at the same instant, and we recognize each other. I am face to face with the boy, who six years earlier killed my wife. I know his face well. I watched from across a courtroom for a full week. He is older now, but I know his face. I am looking at Richard Gibson. There is no doubt about it.

He recognizes me too. Without speaking a word, he is communicating volumes to me. "How can you be here? This doesn't make any sense. What is going on?"

He is also communicating fear to me. He is afraid, and he should be afraid. I am going to kill him.

In an instant, before I can even pull the trigger, Richard Gibson flings his revolver in one direction and Katie in the other.

He screams: "Please don't shoot! The gun isn't even loaded!"

I don't care whether his gun is loaded, though I am quite pleased to now have the hostage clear of my line of fire.

All the hatred I have been carrying for six years is rushing to my head. I am ecstatic, grateful to God for delivering my enemy into my hands. "Thank you, Lord," I say as I squeeze the trigger.

As I squeeze the trigger, though, the expression on Richard Gibson's face changes. He is no longer puzzled. He is terrified, and I recognize that look of terror. I have seen it before.

That horrible frightened look was the last thing I saw a fraction of a second before my sweet Rebecca was taken away from me. I remember it all now. I remember looking to my right and seeing the face of a terrified small boy behind the wheel of a car closing in on Rebecca's door.

My heart softens instantly. I want to unsqueeze the trigger on my rifle, but it is too late. I can't undo the pulling of the trigger.

Then I realize that I have heard no report from my rifle. The gun didn't fire. I take it down from my shoulder and examine it. Looking at the safety on the right side of the receiver, I clearly see that when I pulled back on the lever earlier, I set the safety. I did not release it. I know this gun well. How could I have made such a mistake?

I lay the rifle on the ground, and stand motionless, face to face with Richard Gibson.

Richard is sobbing. "I am so sorry, Mr. Delgado. I killed your wife, and I am so sorry."

Instantly I understand everything. I understand how God could pardon Cain. I understand why God spared Noah and his whole family when the world had become totally corrupt. I understand why God wanted Jonah to lead the people of Nineveh back to Him.

Now I am sobbing too, as I walk toward Richard.

"It's okay, Richard. I forgive you."

Richard Gibson doesn't know what to make of me as I walk toward him with my arms outstretched. I embrace him and hold him close. Over and over he repeats: "I'm so sorry." Over and over I repeat: "I forgive you."

Marty and Katie have moved to the side of the Cessna during this entire exchange. Neither understands what is going on. They remain silent, watching and listening.

I don't know where the words come from as I speak to Richard Gibson.

"Richard, you are not the first person on earth who has killed someone. Cain and Abel were the first two brothers on earth, and Cain killed his brother. Richard, Cain murdered his brother, and God spared him. God spared Cain because he loved him. You are not the worst person who has ever walked on this earth. There was a time when the whole earth became totally corrupt, and even then rather than destroy mankind, God spared one family in order to spare mankind because God loved his creation, man. Richard, there was a place called Nineveh. It was a wicked place, full of evil people, and God loved those people so much that he had a man sent special delivery to them in the belly of a fish just to lead them back to Him.

Richard, it's no accident that you and I are here today. God has brought us together. He has brought us together for both your sake and mine. You need forgiveness, and I need to forgive.

Richard, are you saved?"

"I can't be saved."

"Yes you can, Richard. You can be saved right now. Two thousand years ago God sent his only son to this earth to save anyone and everyone who would believe in him. Do you want God's forgiveness right now?"

"Yes!"

"Then, Richard, pray with me. Lord, I am a sinner. I am an awful sinner who has done awful things, but I know that you sent your son Jesus Christ, to save my soul. I accept your son as my Lord and savior right now, and I thank you for your blessed grace. I know that I can do nothing to erase all the bad I have done, but I also know that your son's death on a cross was payment for all that I have done. Thank you, Lord for the sacrifice you made on my behalf."

Richard repeats this prayer with me.

Then I pray. "Lord, thank you for bringing me to my Nineveh. I forgive Richard completely. Thank you for forgiving my hatred. Thank you for letting me see what I need to see. Thank you for your Son who died for me and Richard Gibson."

Marty and Katie are watching with open mouths. They are trying to understand everything that is happening. Then something powerful happens. They each feel the hair rise on the backs of their necks, and they are each thrown backward against the side of the Civil Air Patrol plane.

Marty exclaims: "What in the world was that?"

Katie answers: "That was the movement of the Holy Spirit."

"The what?" asks Marty.

"That was the Holy Spirit," Katie repeats.

"Have you ever felt that before?" Marty wants to know.

"I have experienced it once before, Marty, and I need to tell you something. I am certain of what we just felt. I am certain that it was meant for both of us. And, I am certain that if we do not act upon what has just happened right now, we will shorty convince ourselves that it was nothing."

"No," said Marty. "That was not 'nothing.' That was something."

"Yes it was Marty, but if we don't acknowledge it now and act upon it, we will convince ourselves over time that it was the wind or that we were just caught up in the moment. We will lose the power of this moment, and I don't want to lose the power of this moment. Do you?"

"No!"

Marty and Katie hold hands as she leads him to accept Jesus Christ as his Lord and savior.

Then Marty asks: "What about you? You said this was for both of us?"

"It is. I think this is about much more than you and that young man getting saved, although that is plenty. I think God is trying to tell us that he has much more in store for us."

"So what do we do now?" asks Marty.

"We ask God to reveal his plans to us."

"And then?"

"Then we believe."

*　*　*　*

At this moment, four police cars come rolling into the airport. They find Richard and me holding each other, and they find Marty and Katie holding hands. All four of us are crying.

The police have no idea who the bad guy is.

Katie, who is obviously not the bad guy, identifies all the players for the police. Richard Gibson is placed in handcuffs. As he is walked toward a police car, he thanks me.

EPILOGUE

It takes several hours for the police to collect statements from Katie, Marty and me. At around eight p.m. we call a cab and go to a favorite barbecue restaurant of mine. Mom and Dad are going to come by with Rachel.

On the way to the restaurant, Katie gets a phone call from her boss, Mr. Owens. Apparently our day's adventures have made the national news. He wants Katie to take the morning off tomorrow, and be sure and wear her CAP uniform to work in the afternoon. The firm will have a photographer there.

Marty needs to figure out how to get tires back on his plane. Katie makes some calls, and is told that CAP will pick up wheels from Marty's hangar and fly them to Abilene in the morning.

Using Katie's cell phone, I call the hospital in Shawnee, and talk with Joe. He is doing fine, and will be released in the morning. Joe wants to know if everything went as planned. I don't understand the question.

We get to the restaurant and eat the most wonderful barbecue I have ever had. The fact that this is the first real food I've had in days probably influences this opinion.

At dinner we talk about ways a person can combine his passion for flying with a passion for serving the Lord. I ask if Katie and Marty have ever heard of Alpha Aviation Mission Outreach, and then tell them all about the organization.

As we are eating dessert, Mom and Dad walk in with Rachel. Rachel runs to me and gives me a hug. Then, she steps back, and says: "Daddy, you smell awful." I guess I do. I haven't bathed or changed clothes since Sunday.

* * * *

I spend the night at Mom and Dad's. After a long, hot shower, I go to my old room to sleep. Instead of crawling into bed, though, I sit in a recliner and pick up Dad's guitar. I strum the only chords I know: G,C, and D, and sing the ditty I sang at the campfire.

Cain killed Able.
This I know,
For the Bible tells me so.

Why's that in the Bible, Joe?
What did God want me to know?

Why? Why? Why? Why?

Why's that in the Bible, Joe?
What did God want me to know?

God is a God of second chances.
God is a God of Love.
God is a God of second chances,
And
God wanted me to know.

Jonah was a tasty dish
in the belly of a fish.

Why's that in the Bible, Joe?
What did God want me to know?

Why? Why? Why? Why?

Why's that in the Bible, Joe?
What did God want me to know?

God is a God of second chances.
God is a God of Love.
God is a God of second chances,
And
God wanted me to know.

Noah built a big old boat.
Didn't know if it would float.

Why's that in the Bible, Joe?
What did God want me to know?

Why? Why? Why? Why?

Why's that in the Bible, Joe?
What did God want me to know?

God is a God of second chances.
God is a God of Love.
God is a God of second chances,
And
God wanted me to know.

Jesus died upon a tree.
He rose again on day three.

Why's that in the Bible, Joe?
What did God want me to know?

Why? Why? Why? Why?

Why's that in the Bible, Joe?
What did God want me to know?

God is a God of second chances.
God is a God of Love.
God is a God of second chances,
And
God wanted me to know.

*   *   *   *

One week later, Joe prepares himself a cup of coffee, and sits down in his favorite chair for his evening Bible reading. He reads his scriptures for the night, finishes his coffee, and picks up a framed photo of his wife, Beverly. Joe kisses the picture, and places it back on the table. He says: "Okay, Lord, I'm ready." Joe closes his eyes and goes home to be with the Lord.

The End

CPSIA information can be obtained at www.ICGtesting.com
Printed in the USA
LVOW060558250412

279062LV00002B/4/P